# SHARED IN THE OFFICE AND BEYOND

## 10 HOTWIFE JOURNEY COLLECTION

## LACEY CROSS

TWISTED ROSE
· PUBLISHING ·

TWISTED ROSE PUBLISHING

# CONTENTS

# PREFACE

Thanks for picking up my 10-story hotwife bundle. These stories all follow Miranda as she and her husband navigate her first-time hotwife experiences. She starts with her bosses and continues on with her agreeing to be a birthday gift for various people.

Along the way, Miranda realizes she has a BDSM kink and many of the stories explore BDSM themes while she's experiencing her hotwife escapades. I've written 14 books with Miranda, as well as many erotica shorts. These first 10 books are the order I'd recommend someone read because there is an overall journey for Miranda through all the books I've written for her.

She's the character I've written the most and I hope you enjoy reading her stories as much as I loved writing them.

Lacey

# SERVICING THE SENIOR PARTNER

# CHAPTER 1

*Will my boss fire me for being late too often?* I glance at the clock on my phone as I dash out of my house. I'm running late for the third time this week, and it's only Wednesday. *Shit, the guys I work for are going to be angry.*

I'm an administrative assistant at a small legal firm, and I work for three—soon to be four—sexy lawyers. Whoever decided that lawyers had to be attractive should get a lifetime achievement award. If I'd been searching for a job with eye-candy potential, I'd have stumbled into the perfect position. I'm not kidding when I say they're hot. I've heard all my bosses talk about their morning gym routines, and I'm pretty sure they all work out every day.

The big boss, Mr. Jacobs, is probably in his mid-fifties and he's the oldest of the three—and the most intimidating. His paralegal is on vacation, so I've been helping with extra duties. I'm not a paralegal so it's nerve wracking. I could make horrible mistakes on legal paperwork, but so far no one has complained—other than about my attendance.

My lack of sleep is to blame for my tardiness. Last night I went to bed at a decent time but laid there fantasizing about fucking someone other than my husband and I got so worked up, it was hard to fall asleep. And after I finally fell asleep, I had a crazy sex dream involving my BOSS and I woke up wet. I'm never going to live this down if I tell Jon about it.

I reminisce about the dream the entire drive to work—*god, it was hot*—but push the thought to the back of my brain as I scurry into the building. It's possible no one will notice I'm ten minutes late again.

No such luck. I hang my coat up in the tiny employee break room and attempt to sneak to my desk. When I turn the corner, Mr. Jacobs is standing right by my workstation and putting a stack of files on it.

His salt and pepper hair looks recently trimmed. He's wearing a full navy suit, which means he has a deposition this morning. The nerves in my stomach jump at the sight of his white shirt and dark brown Foulard tie underneath the navy fabric. Pretty sure my fantasy last night included that exact tie, and not in a Fifty Shades type of way. I didn't even know what a Foulard tie was until I started working at the office, but I'm now a fan. Dreamland Mr. Jacobs was in a full suit while I was under his desk giving him a blowjob. Seeing him in a similar outfit this morning is thrilling and awkward.

"Miranda, you're late again," Mr. Jacobs scolds when he spots me heading towards my desk, and he sighs heavily.

His stern voice, coupled with his starring role in my recent dream, creates a flush through my entire body and a renewed realization that I'm still wet. I squirm and shift from foot to foot, trying to avoid eye contact because I sense my face is pink.

"I'm sorry. Things are crazy at home right now. It won't happen again," I rush to explain and trip over my tongue a little. Except, I know it will happen again. It's life, shit happens and everyone is late to work occasionally. It's just bad timing for it to happen three times in a row when Mr. Jacobs is paying attention to my schedule.

He grumbles a little and explains what to do with the files on my desk. I want him to leave before I die of embarrassment. Just being close to him is turning me on, and I keep glancing at the way the suit molds to his shoulders as he's explaining my duties for the morning.

When Mr. Jacobs turns to go, he takes two steps and announces, "By the way, the color pink suits you," before he heads down the hallway to his office.

I immediately freak out. Oh my god, he noticed I was blushing! I'm sure he thought it was because I was late, right? The panic sets in and I wonder if it's time to find a new job. I really love my job, but now the big boss thinks I'm flighty and a horrible worker. What am I going to do?

I'm about to pick up my phone and text my best friend, Dina, and spew my thoughts to her when I glance down and realize I'm wearing a pink button-down shirt paired with a tight black pencil skirt and high heels. *Oh jeez, I'm an idiot.* I plop back in my office chair and go over the conversation in my head again. He's never complimented me before. *Maybe he felt bad for snapping at me?* Deciding I've made a fool enough of myself this morning, I flip my computer on and tell myself it's time to buckle down and tackle the files.

My brain has a different plan and doesn't want to work. I alternate between thinking about Mr. Jacobs and then going back to something my husband recently said.

My husband, Jon, and I had an interesting weekend. We've been having long talks every night, so I've been falling asleep later than normal. It's throwing off my entire schedule and jacking up my mornings while I rush around trying to get ready for work. A few months ago, he expressed a sexual fantasy of his was for me to have sex with someone else and then come home and tell him every detail. I initially laughed at him, assuming it was a joke, because he wasn't advocating for him to sleep around as well, but he swore he was serious. I told him I would consider it and dropped the subject.

When he brought up the idea of me sleeping with someone outside of the marriage again, I was horny and agreed to the idea. Just the thought of me doing it with someone else turned him into a wild beast on Sunday night, which is why I was late Monday morning. Now he's been non-stop talking about it every night and urging me to find someone hot to fuck ASAP.

He and I married somewhat young these days. I was twenty, and he's five years older than I am. We've made it past eight years of marriage and I recently turned twenty-eight. Everyone jokes about the seven-year itch in a marriage, and I don't think it's a myth. Jon and I have been in a sex slump the last year. We're both working full time and he gets home three hours after I do. By the time we eat dinner and spend a bit of time together, it's bedtime for me. We're still having sex regularly, but it's less spicy and more routine. Definitely not what I expected at twenty-eight when I'm just heading into my prime sexual years.

This is all my husband's fault. Everything was fine until he told me to go find someone else to fuck. Now it's causing awkwardness at work. Mr. Jacobs has always been attractive, but my brain made him off-limits since I'm married. I'd never considered him as anything but my sexy boss. But Jon pushing me to think of someone else to screw made me reconsider—which led to my dream.

Two hours later I noticed an internal email ping from Mr. Jacobs titled RE: Attendance. Oh shit, I really am busted. I open the email and he tells me to stop by his office after work to discuss my habitual tardiness. I hear his voice in my head as I skim the message and, while I feel like I'm in trouble and this meeting isn't a good thing, the thought of him saying "habitual tardiness" in his strict voice is erotic.

# CHAPTER 2

By lunchtime, I'm still worked up and horny. This better not be how all my days go now that I'm supposed to be considering who to sleep with. My brain is basically contemplating every man in the office, and I'd fuck all three of the lawyers I work for in a heartbeat. If I had a preference, it would be Mr. Jacobs because he has that hot dad vibe going on. Sometimes I enjoy pretending to be a bad girl, but it never quite works with my husband when he's only five years older than me.

I'm alone in the break room and decide now is the only chance I'm going to get to talk to Dina about my issues. She works evenings so by the time I get off work she can't take my phone call. We mostly communicate via text during the day or if I occasionally call her during my lunch break.

When Dina answers, I blurt out all my problems, leaving nothing out. She already knows about Jon's desire for me to sleep with other people, but I hadn't yet told her I agreed to the idea. My lunch break isn't long, so I rush and explain it all and conclude by telling her I'm now having inappropriate fantasies about my bosses.

Right about then is when I realize that Mr. Jacobs and one of the other lawyers, Mr. Parks, are standing outside the doorway with stricken faces, as if they had intended to come into the break room but stopped.

*Ooooh, fuck.* I tell Dina I have to go without an explanation and end the call. I gather my lunch quickly and silently, and rush out the door past the two gape-mouthed lawyers. Well, I probably just got myself fired. It was a pleasant job while it lasted.

I'm numb and stare at my computer screen blankly for half an hour. Should I leave before someone talks to me? Something flashes and jolts me out of my slump. We use an instant messenger program on our computer for informal messages to each other. If you want a record of something, you email it since the email service backs up our correspondence. Otherwise we're fine using instant messenger.

The message is from Mr. Jacobs and simply says, "I think we could help you with your problem."

*Wait, WHAT?* My pussy zings alive once again. Is he suggesting what my cooch assumes he is?

I quickly respond, "What problem are you talking about?"

The messenger program tells you when someone is typing and Mr. Jacobs is either typing something incredibly long, or he paused mid thought. My heart races while I wait for his response.

His answer is shorter than I expected. "You can do any of us whenever you want."

*OH... MY... GOD.* Of course, my brain put his voice in my head when he said that, so imagining him whispering that to me added an extra flavor to the message. My lady parts buzz in approval and a splash of wetness leaks out. I'm tempted to go to the restroom and finger myself with his voice in my head, telling me I can do him whenever I want. That's orgasm-worthy material right there.

Oh, but he's probably expecting a response! I type and tell him I need to check on something. I know that sounds odd and cagey, but

I pull out my phone and text my husband. "Can I fuck Mr. Jacobs at work?"

Jon's response is almost instantaneous. "Tonight?"

I'm not sure how to respond since I don't know the answer. I just type "maybe" with a little emoji smiley face.

He responds with a thumbs up, an eggplant, and simply says, "I expect a full report when I get home."

*Holy shit, can I actually do this?* I press my pussy lips against the chair and wiggle around for friction. I've got an itch that needs scratching, and Mr. Jacobs could take care of it.

I flip my attention back to my computer screen and message my boss, "Are you free after work?"

He immediately responds, "Yes, right after our meeting about your tardiness."

*Ooooh, hell, yeah.* My fingers are shaking and I'm breathing fast as I type, "I look forward to it."

Mr. Jacobs doesn't respond, so I'm left to work for a few more hours until my shift is over. I'm pretty sure I'm getting nothing done this afternoon. My brain wants to replay my under-the-desk fantasy while I daydream about my upcoming meeting.

# CHAPTER 3

My shift finally ends and the receptionist, Cindy, says goodnight to me. Our firm is so small that the two of us are the only staff when the paralegal isn't around. I wait a few minutes to make sure she doesn't come back for anything she forgot. While I kill time, I text my husband to tell him I have a meeting with the boss in a minute. I include a taco and eggplant emoji, just in case he's dense.

Once I'm certain Cindy isn't returning, I head to Mr. Jacobs's office. I knock on the door and he bids me to enter. He's sitting behind his desk as I walk in and close the door behind me. Neither of us speaks for a moment, and my entire body tingles while I wait for him to say something.

"Have a seat, Miranda. We need to talk." Mr. Jacobs's voice is neutral, and he doesn't seem angry. The thought crossed my mind that he might fire me. *I hope he fucks me first.*

I sit down and cross my legs, letting my pencil skirt slide up past my knees. Mr. Jacobs glances at my legs, so I know I hit my target with my chosen posture.

"I'm really sorry I was late today. I, uh, didn't sleep well last night." Halfway through my explanation, I realize he knows exactly why I didn't sleep well last night, since that was part of my explanation about my fantasy to Dina. I am not sure I could flush a brighter pink, and the temperature in the room increases by a few degrees.

"We can talk about your attendance later. Does your husband know you are staying late?"

*Oh, now that's interesting. Does he want to know if I have permission to screw him?* I give him a soft smile and smooth my long brown hair over my shoulder. "My husband is fully supportive of me working overtime tonight, or any night it's required."

Mr. Jacobs pauses and carefully words his next question, "What if the other lawyers require overtime as well?"

My head spins. *Does he mean at once?* My pussy clenches at the thought of all three of them stuffing my holes. I mean, I have three holes and there are three of them, right? The fourth partner doesn't join the firm for another week. But Jon never mentioned a gang bang fantasy, so I better rein that thought in.

I'm hesitant as I reply, "I am fine with overtime by anyone, as long as it's only one person needing overtime at a time."

He and I are clearly talking about the same thing. I'm about ready to stop with the double entendre speech and tell him I'm down to fuck all of them as long as it's not a gang bang, when he stands up and breaks my concentration because the front of his trousers is bulging. He's turned on and hard.

"Then come over here so we can discuss your tardiness."

My heart leaps into my throat. *Yes! Let's get this party started.* Uncrossing my legs, I stand up slowly. I'm nervous and a little unsteady on my feet. I sashay towards him slowly, hoping that it looks sexy and pause a foot from him. My brain is a gooey mess of possibilities. What is he going to tell me to do? Is he really going to punish me? He could demand I apologize and go down on him. My wet pussy tells me I'm down for all of those scenarios.

Mr. Jacobs's calculating eyes regard my breasts for a moment before he reaches out to unbutton my shirt. As each button slips open, the cool air hits my newly exposed skin. I'm not cold, but I shiver. I tucked my blouse into my skirt this morning and he doesn't pull the shirt out. He leaves it tucked in, but pushes it open to reveal more of my stomach and chest. I'm wearing a simple white cotton bra and mentally curse myself for not being the type of girl who wears sexy underclothes every day. If I knew how this day was going to end, I would have made smarter choices this morning.

He trails a finger over each mound of breast and traces my hard nipple through the cotton. I gasp and sway towards him a little. I haven't been this turned on in a very, very long time. The dampness of my panties tells me I'm ready for action.

Instead of removing any more of my clothes, he turns me around and pushes me against his mahogany desk. He bends me over the top, pressing my breasts against the hard surface. I'm laying at his workstation right in front of where he normally sits. I realize he pushed his keyboard to the side before I got into the room, almost as if he planned on me being in this position. The cold surface of the desk cools my flushed skin and I feel him unzip my skirt from the side. I should wear looser skirts, more suited for this type of "work" in the future.

The logistics of my skirt don't phase him and he easily pushes it down to pool at my ankles. I feel a moment of embarrassment over my days-of-the-week panties. They were a gag gift from my husband and I love them, but this morning I tossed on Sunday because Wednesday was missing from my drawer and I was running too late to hunt for them.

Mr. Jacobs chuckles under his breath, and I assume he's finding my Sunday panties amusing. I squirm my ass a little, wishing he'd pull my panties down and fuck me. But I'm rewarded with a sharp spank instead, hard enough to make my teeth ring, and I gasp in shock. *Oh shit, I guess we're going with the punishment option?*

"Are you going to be late again tomorrow?" Mr. Jacobs's voice is harsh and his ragged breathing turns me on even more. I imagine how I look to him right now, and I try to memorize the emotions and sounds so I can recount them later to Jon.

I'm half tempted to be naughty and tell him I'll be late whenever I want, but his stern dad hand is a little painful so I play it safe. Trying to sound contrite, I vow, "I'm sorry. I won't be late tomorrow. I swear."

He doesn't respond, but rubs the sting out of my ass cheek and runs his fingers over my bush, tickling it through the cotton fabric. *Mmm, now that's more like it.* I press against his hand, knowing my panties are wet and there is no hiding how much I want him inside of me.

Mr. Jacobs peels my panties down but leaves them at my knees, while forcing my legs to spread wider to give him better access. I hear the clink of his metal belt buckle and a zipper being pulled down.

Assuming he is going to ram his cock into me, I brace myself against the desk. But instead of his penis, his fingers probe my hole. I moan as he pushes two digits inside of me, and he gently finger fucks me for a moment. I'm fine with being punished like this any day, but his fingers make me want more.

I wiggle my ass again, hoping he'll take the hint, and he moves his slippery fingers to rub circles around my clit. Moaning, I realize I'm already close to an orgasm. I've been so turned on all day, and this whole punishment fantasy and being bent over the desk is my number one office daydream. I can't believe this is actually happening. My boss's fingers are flicking my bean with expertise. He's obviously gotten plenty of practice on servicing women over the years.

Is he going to want to hear that Mr. Jacobs knows exactly how to touch me? Maybe he'll want a visual demonstration of my position on the desk. Thinking about retelling all of this to Jon later is crazy hot, but all I want right now is a hard cock pounding inside of me until I can't think anymore.

Mr. Jacobs speeds up his fingers and I gasp. I won't last long at this rate and I want more. I look over my shoulder at him and plead, "I need you inside of me."

He immediately replaces his hand with the tip of his shaft, and I groan as it parts my lips. He's nudging my hole, and then removing his rod, and then prodding it again, but a little harder. *Jesus Christ, if he doesn't shove that in me soon...*

I squeal as he thrusts his cock straight to my core, ramming into me and pressing against my ass. It's been over eight years since I've had anything but my husband or a toy inside of me. Mr. Jacobs is thicker than my husband, though possibly shorter. He's stretching my hole, and I feel stuffed. If he's a shorter length, it doesn't matter. The fullness is awesome, and he's hitting nerve endings I didn't know I had.

He doesn't give me time to adjust to his size. He pulls out fully and slams back inside repeatedly. Each thrust forces my chest to rub the desk and my pert nipples slide against the hard wood and add extra zing to the plowing of my pussy. This is dirty, slutty, and I love it.

He speeds up the pace, and he's breathing heavily and groaning. My legs quiver and I'm edging close to my orgasm. His heavy balls whack against my clit with each thrust, and I try to push back towards him to force him in deeper. He puts his hands on the desk on both sides of me so he can bend over slightly as he shortens his plunges.

Oh shit, he's hitting the good spot deep inside repeatedly, hard and fast from this position. I repeat "oh my god" over and over as he jackhammers against me. I close my eyes as I peak and shatter with release. My cave walls shudder and he moans and stiffens behind me. Waves of pleasure wash over me and my pussy milks him as he comes.

He pulls out and sits down in his office chair with a groan. I stay right where he left me. It's going to take a moment for me to collect my thoughts. I can feel his cum leaking out of me and I'm curious what he tastes like. I might have to sample that before I clean up fully.

The squishy feeling makes me realize that Jon and I didn't talk about safe sex practices. So this was probably dumb of me, but it's too late now. I'll have to see what he thinks tonight, but for now I'm loving having another man's jizz inside of me.

Mr. Jacobs pulls my panties up and I take that as my cue to move off his desk. I stand up and stumble slightly because my legs are like jelly, but quickly right myself and stand still until my legs want to support me again. He's adjusting his trousers and straightening his clothes, so I do the same. He finishes before I do and watches me.

"So Miranda, no regrets?" He sounds happier than I've ever heard him, relaxed and pleasant.

I giggle a little and glance at him. "No regrets. I loved it."

"Mr. Parks mentioned he might have some extra work for you tomorrow, if you are interested."

My pussy is more than satisfied, but a slight twinge of excitement darts through me at the thought of another cock.

"I'll let him know I'm available. And if you ever have any extra work again, please let me know." I grin at him. This job just became the best place of employment ever. I might literally get fucked every single day.

Mr. Jacobs laughs. "Don't worry, I'll have plenty of work for you."

I reach over and kiss his cheek before leaving. As I'm gathering the stuff from my desk, I write a quick note to Mr. Parks to tell him I'm available for overtime tomorrow. I slip it under his door as I leave.

I don't check my phone until I get to the car and Jon has been blowing it up with messages, eager for all the details. Feeling too relaxed and happy for a long texting session. I simply reply that I'm on my way home and include a firework and party face emoji. That's all he's going to get for now.

As I'm driving home, I think about the three lawyers in the office and a warm fuzzy feeling overwhelms me. This relationship is going to be awesome. I'm going to take care of all of them, and in return I'm going to have more sex than I know what to do with. My cooch gives a little buzz to tell me she knows exactly what to do with all the sex, and she's hoping for more tonight after I tell Jon how my session with the senior partner went.

My driveway is empty when I get home and it's still a couple of hours before Jon will be off work, but I'm excited to see him. I glance at my phone and fall more in love with my husband when I see a text that says, "Don't shower."

I'm also considering being late to work more often since it worked out so well today.

The End

# DELIGHTING THE BOSS

# CHAPTER 1

When I get to work on Thursday, I'm a bundle of nerves. The last 24 hours have been a wild ride. First it started with me accidentally blabbing in front of two of my bosses about my sexually inappropriate fantasies involving one of them. Then, in a crazy twist of fate, I ended up being fucked on the desk of the Senior Partner, Mr. Jacobs. I'm still hot and bothered about my day yesterday.

I thought my sex life with my husband, Jon, was mostly satisfying, but what happened with Mr. Jacobs yesterday was beyond my expectations. Jon is totally on board with all of this—and in fact, it was his idea. Last night we had amazing shower sex after I told him all the details about my encounter with Mr. Jacobs. Afterwards, I went to bed a very satisfied woman. Something about being used by my boss thrills me to my core. But I have three bosses and I was told they all would request me to work "overtime." when possible.

This morning, I'm all aflutter again because of a note I slipped under Mr. Parks's office door before I left work yesterday, telling him I would be available to provide services today. I don't know what result to expect, but I'm wet and ready for whatever this day brings.

Before I get out of the car, I give a last glance in the rearview mirror to make sure my long brown hair is presentable. Smoothing down my blue shirt, I ensure it's fully tucked into my black skirt. I love wearing skirts to work, but today I wore a looser one after I learned my mistake from wearing a tighter one the previous day. I want Mr. Parks to push it up, if he wants.

The office is mostly empty and the receptionist, Cindy, reminds me that the partners have an early meeting and are all in the conference room. I breathe a sigh of relief since I wasn't sure how to act around Mr. Parks this morning. The meeting means I won't randomly run into him in the hallway for a bit. I slide into my desk chair and boot up my computer.

Oh shit, what if they're meeting about me? My heart rate speeds up and I flush. If this continues to be a regular office thing, how could they not be talking about me? Ugh, is Mr. Jacobs telling them exactly how he fucked me? My pussy clenches at the thought of Mr. Jacobs and his desk, and I switch gears to think about what Mr. Parks might ask of me. The delicious unknown causes a shivering tingle to run down the back of my neck and the hairs to stand up on my arms. It's going to be torture to wait until after work.

# CHAPTER 2

Their meeting in the conference room runs extra long, but I can occasionally detect large barks of laughter through the door. My desk is down a corridor and around a corner from the conference room, so for me to hear laughter means it's incredibly loud. I finish one of my files and take it up to Cindy at the front for mailing. While I'm standing there making idle small talk, the three partners and an absolutely stunning stranger come from the conference area.

The unfamiliar man is a little over six feet tall, with broad shoulders tucked into a navy business suite. I would estimate his age in the late 30s. He's skin is a rich brown and when he smiles his eyes crinkle in a friendly way and his straight white teeth light up his face. It's pretty uncommon I meet someone who I'm this immediately attracted to, but as the group of four men walks up to the receptionist's desk, my whole body lights on fire with tingles. *Who is this god-like creature?*

Mr. Jacobs introduces the new guy to us. "Cindy and Miranda, I'd like to introduce you to our fourth partner starting on Monday. Everyone, this is Mr. Daniels."

Mr. Daniels stops to shake my hand and when our palms touch, I swear sparks fly between us. He doesn't seem affected, so it's probably only on my end. Or maybe I'm so worked up from yesterday with

Mr. Jacobs and then the thought of what is in store for me today with Mr. Parks, I might be a match waiting to be lit from any little thing.

I stay at the front desk, vibrating with excitement while the men chat for a few minutes. My legs are shaking and if I attempted to return to my desk right now, it would end up appearing as if I was doing a hangover walk of shame from a night of excess. It's better if I stay and pretend I had more to say to Cindy until they leave. I keep expecting someone to make a comment or make some sign that they were talking about me in the meeting or give me a knowing glance.

Nothing happens, to my disappointment, and the men break apart. The new guy waves goodbye to us on the way out the door, and everyone else except Mr. Parks heads to their respective offices. Mr. Parks is in his mid-40s and on the slender side. Salt and pepper short brown hair, hazel eyes, and glasses complete the aspect of a nerdy lawyer. Normally I wouldn't say his type was hot, but his confidence, along with how I know he's incredibly fit and muscular under his clothes, gives him the extra push from attractive to hot. The only reason I know he's fit and muscular is because of our occasional casual days at the office where everyone comes in wearing jeans and a t-shirt. He might be thinner than my tastes, but he wears it well and I plan on being all over him soon enough.

Mr. Parks pauses and addresses Cindy and me. "I'm running to the deli down the street and will bring you both something back for lunch."

When he walks out the door without giving me any special attention, I deflate. Maybe he doesn't intend to ask me to stick around after work today? There was no note on my desk, no emails, and no recognition of my offer to stay late. Hell, it's possible Mr. Jacobs was wrong and the entire office isn't planning to stuff my muff. I'm not dumb, I literally work for a law firm and this seems like a sexual harassment lawsuit waiting to happen if I wasn't a willing participant in this little reverse harem. I'm honestly surprised Mr. Jacobs didn't talk to me about this, but I'm guessing he was too busy pounding my pussy to think of it.

UGH, what if they talked about it in the meeting today and changed their minds? I stew about this uncomfortable development while I attempt to get more work done. My pussy is dripping wet and I really hope the men don't want to back out of our arrangement. I don't know if I want to go back to just sleeping with my husband now that this lifestyle is an option. And where else am I going to find three—possibly four—super hot, willing guys that I trust?

Cindy eventually brings me a bag with my name on it from the deli down the street. The family-owned deli puts the individual names on the bags when doing a group order, which is a pleasant touch. But I didn't actually tell Mr. Parks what I wanted, so I was curious about what he ordered. But I'm a bundle of nerves and not sure I'm hungry for lunch. The longer I'm at work with no information about staying late, the more tense and upset I become. Was this all really a bad idea? My drenched panties tell me otherwise, but I don't enjoy waiting on tenterhooks all day. I want to be less confused and feel more desirable.

The lunch bag is sitting on a file I need, so I pick it up and give it a toss to the other end of my desk. When it lands, a soft thud on the wood indicates the sandwich isn't the only item in the bag. *Uh, what?* I grab the sack and peek inside. There is a deli sandwich wrapped up like normal, but along with it is a small box about the size of a jeweler's ring box. I snatch it out and peer down the hall to make sure no one is nearby. My desk is mostly hidden around a corner from the main part of the office, but that doesn't mean people don't occasionally come down this direction, either to pass by me on the way to the conference room, or to talk to me.

Seeing that I'm alone, I pry the lid off the little box. Inside is a folded note hiding whatever is underneath. When I pick up the paper, a bright purple, egg-shaped sex toy peeks out from a piece of tissue paper. The egg is covered in a nubby silicone sleeve with a ring attached to it, so if you stick it up your twat, you can't lose it since you would just fish it out with the ring. My breath catches and my angst immediately drains from my body while a thrill zings straight to my clit. Holy shit, what if Cindy had opened the wrong bag? The audacity of having her deliver it to me is so fucking hot. I wish I could go to Mr. Parks, lie on his desk, and tell him to fuck me hard right now.

But first, I better read the note. I unfold it and notice it's done on company letterhead and printed out, which means he sent it to the printer in the central part of the office. It's the only printer filled with company letterhead.

Miranda,

The fully charged vibrating egg should last over 3 hours on the lowest setting. At 1 p.m. I want you to slide it inside of you and keep it on low. I require your assistance in my office at 4 p.m. sharp. Don't wait for Cindy to leave. Just come and knock on my door. You must not orgasm before our appointment time. If you feel you are getting close, remove the egg for 5 minutes, cool down, and then stick it back in.

Sincerely,

Mr. Parks

When I'm finished, I fold the note and stare at the purple egg. If this thing were alive, I swear it would wink at me with a mocking glance. All morning I believed Mr. Parks was ignoring me or not interested, when in reality he had this trick up his sleeve the entire time. Everything about the note, the letterhead, the egg, along with the directions, is almost more than my frazzled sex-crazed mind can handle. I thought Mr. Jacobs was the sexiest man in the office, but Mr. Parks just blew Mr. Jacobs out of the competition with this stunt. This is by far THE HOTTEST thing that has happened to me in my life. Add the twist of Cindy delivering the bag, and I'm ready to come all over his cock this very moment. I am hot, bothered, and so down to fuck right now it's unbelievable.

I grind my pussy back and forth in my chair, trying to relieve the incredible ache I have, and I glance at the clock on my computer. Ugh, it's only motherfucking 11:30 a.m. What in the fuck am I going to do for another hour and a half before I can use the egg? How am I supposed to get any work done?

I pout and glare at the egg for a few more seconds and get a brilliant idea. Picking up my phone, I glance around to make sure I'm still alone before positioning the folded note next to the egg in the box, and then snap a picture. I unfold the note and snap a closeup to reveal the writing. I text my husband, attach both pictures, and simply say, "Look what I have."

Jon doesn't disappoint and within a few minutes he texts back with five fire emojis, but nothing else. I glance at the clock again, and it says 11:35 a.m. This is going to be a hellishly long afternoon.

# CHAPTER 3

At 12:55 I slip into the restroom to insert the egg because I can't wait a minute longer. My breasts ache and my poor, swollen lady parts beg to be stuffed. The egg has a tiny silicone button you press to turn it on, and one press puts it on the lowest setting. The entire thing is waterproof. I put my foot on the toilet seat, pull up my skirt, and push aside my panties to insert the buzzing egg. I get immediate relief from it sliding into my wet hole, but quickly realize that this is going to be difficult to handle. Even on the lowest setting, the vibrations are intense on my sensitive skin. I've been ready to fuck for over two hours now, so how do I expect to sit there with this vibrating inside of me for the next three hours?

I stroll back to my desk, and when I sit down, the egg shifts higher up my cave of wonders, causing a small gasp to escape from the pleasure. Squirming in my chair, I enjoy the vibration deep inside. I glance at the clock and it says 1:03 p.m. Yeah, this is going to suck... in such a deliciously erotic way.

At 1:10 p.m, I decide this is all mind over matter. I'm going to get so focused on my work, the time will fly. That works for about 20 minutes until I notice I'm rocking in my chair and breathing heavier than normal. I have to stop and evaluate how close I am to an orgasm because it's several steps down the hall to the restroom to remove it. Deeming it safe, I resume working, which really means I am staring at a wall daydreaming about all the ways I want Mr. Parks to fuck me. Eventually I turn my desk fan on and point it straight at my face because I'm starting to overheat.

At 1:30 p.m, Mr. Parks comes by to hand me some files. He paused at my desk and looks me over with a critical eye, but doesn't put the files down.

"Having a productive afternoon, Miranda? You're a bit flushed."

"Uh, everything is going fine, sir. I'm just finishing some paper-work." My face is beet red and I attempt to avoid his eyes.

I also realize I'm about two minutes from coming with him stand-ing there, and I need to get this egg out of me right now. I stand up quickly and try to walk around Mr. Parks, but he blocks my path.

"Going somewhere? I want to discuss these files with you." He grins at me, with a sexy evil glint in his eye.

I pant, "I'm going to the restroom and will be right back."

He doesn't step aside and actively moves in my direction when I try to get around him.

"Look at me, Miranda," he demands.

I'm literally about to orgasm at any moment. My pussy spasms as I meet his gaze.

"I want you to come with me to my office. Right now."

When he says that, I can't control myself and I orgasm. My body shivers, and I throw a hand against the wall as waves of pleasure wash through me. A long, soft moan escapes and I'm left gasping for breath as I come down from the peak. This toy is agony in my sensitive hole and I need to take it out and give my poor pussy a break.

Mr. Parks sighs in disappointment. "Well, I guess you have to wait until 4 p.m. now." He lays the files on my desk and leaves without another word.

I watch him retreat and make a dash for the restroom. Once I'm in there, I pull out the egg with a groan and switch it off. I perch on the toilet seat lid, while my brain is a gigantic pile of mush. Oh my God. I can't believe what just happened. I'm not sure I can handle another round with the toy, but what happens if I go to his room without it in? Maybe I can sit for a while without it and then put it back in right before 4 without him noticing. There is no way in hell I can do two more hours with this egg and how turned on I already am, but I'm afraid he won't fuck me if I show up without the egg or he somehow finds out I don't have it in.

I camp out in the restroom for a good 10 minutes before returning the egg to my sodden hole, and hope for the best while I go back to my desk to get more work done. I'm not sure whether I hate him or love him at this moment. This plan is another level of torture that I've never experienced before. Back at my desk, I text out my woes to Jon and tell him I just orgasmed while standing up in front of Mr. Parks.

He texts back, "poor kitten" with a little evil grinning devil and flame emoji, which leads me to think he's not sorry for me in the slightest. I'll talk to him tonight about his lack of sympathy. I sigh and attempt to concentrate on the files Mr. Parks brought me, but the lines blur in front of my eyes as my brain runs a movie of him fucking me against a wall in his office.

I'm distracted, but notice my instant messenger flash on my computer. I pop it open and it's a message from Mr. Parks.

"Are you ready to help me in my office yet?"

*Oooh, is he offering an early treat again?* My fingers shake as I type back, "Yes, please."

"Then come here immediately."

I reply that I'm on my way while I mentally do a victory dance. Thank God I won't have to wait until after work.

# CHAPTER 4

I knock on Mr. Parks's door, thankful that Cindy wasn't at her desk when I traveled through the lobby. No one needs her counting the exact minutes I'm in here alone with Mr. Parks. He tells me to enter, and as I open the door, I close and lock it behind me. I haven't been in his office that often, but I knew he kept his pet bearded dragon at work. I glance over at the glass aquarium and spot the tan lizard chewing on the last bit of a leafy green. Looks like someone had a snack recently.

Mr. Parks clears his throat to draw my attention back to him. He's sitting in his chair behind his desk, and smack in the middle of the desk is a huge pump bottle of lube. Uh... what do we need lube for? My brain blanks out and my pussy clenches on the vibrating egg. I'm getting close to another orgasm and that bottle of lube scares and excites me. There's only one reason I can come up with that we would need it, and this is uncharted territory for me. Maybe I needed to have that conversation with Mr. Jacobs after all and discuss hard limits, but I admit to myself that I'm incredibly intrigued and so close to coming again that I'm not sure I care which hole he stuffs. I just want his cock however I can get it.

"Come over here, take off your skirt and panties, and I want you to bend over the desk in front of me."

Holy shit, this is hot. I didn't picture being fucked on every desk in the office, but this will be the second one now. When you think about it, there aren't many private areas in the building in the middle of the day. It would make sense they keep bending me over their desks. And really, I'm not complaining. All four can bend me over any surface and I'll just say "please" and "thank you" at the end.

I hasten over to his side of the desk, drop my skirt and panties to the floor, and kick my shoes off at the same time. I'm naked from the waist down and ready for the action to start. He scoots his chair back and I move in front of him. I hear his belt buckle clink and his pants unzip while I'm leaning over and getting settled.

Mr. Parks croons softly as I present myself. "God, that's a pretty sight."

Assuming he can see the egg inside of me, I wiggle my ass around to entice him. Closing my eyes, I angle closer to the desk until I'm resting my head against the cool surface. I'm breathless with anticipation and I hope this doesn't hurt. I guess now the plan with the egg makes total sense. I'm too turned on and hyper-aware of any touch, so everything he does is going to feel amazing.

His hands brush against my pussy lips and I moan as he strokes my clit gently.

"Oh, you're all turned on, aren't you? Do you want me to take care of that for you?"

I moan out, "yes," while he massages my clit in circles. I'm seriously going to come any second, and I'm afraid if I do, he'll stop and tell me to return at 4 p.m. again. He stands up and leans over me to grab the bottle of lube by my head. My long brown hair is in a neat low ponytail today and he uses a hand to tug on it a little, forcing my head off the desk.

He chuckles to himself. "Oh, nice. Something to hold on to." He releases my hair so he can use both hands on the bottle of lube.

Should I tell him I've never done it in the ass before? This seems like an important fact he needs to know before we begin.

"Uh, Mr. Parks?" I'm hesitant and not sure exactly how to word this.

I hear the bottle pump and his inhaled breath as I imagine he's applying lube to himself. He replies with a distracted, "Hmm?"

"I've never done this."

Behind me, he goes silent, as if he stopped moving. "You've never been fucked in the ass before? How about with a finger?"

I peep out a small "no," and try not to be embarrassed.

He sighs heavily. "Oh, baby girl. You're going to love it, but this saddens me. I really wanted to fuck that pretty little ass of yours, but now I think we're going to need some training sessions to work up to it."

*Woah, what?* Training sessions? I imagine him sticking various objects of increasing size in my ass. I grind my pubic bone against the desk and pant as I try to cut off the orgasm I almost have from the visual.

He chuckles, and the squeak from the lube pump tells me he's using it again. I don't know what to expect, but a cold drip of lube hits my asshole and I squirm, trying to move away.

"Hey, hold on. Just relax and let me work it in. I won't do much today. This is just a small taste."

A finger touches my asshole as he smears lube all around. This is erotic and dirty, and with the buzzing egg still in my pussy, I'm more willing to experiment than I normally would have been. He continues to work lube all around and I unwind. This isn't so bad.

As soon as I relax, he exerts pressure as he slowly inserts a finger into my ass. He works the digit in and out, slightly, just to lube me up better. One finger doesn't hurt and actually is pretty nice once I adjust to the odd feeling of fullness.

He gets a little more into it, pressing his finger deeper as the lubrication works its magic. I have a wild thought that, thank God, he's got smaller fingers for a guy. I almost laugh aloud except right at that moment he pulls the vibrating egg out and I moan instead. He positions himself behind me, and the hair on his bare legs tickles me, which means he'd let his pants drop to the floor.

Without warning, the head of his cock nudges my wet hole and as soon as he knows he found it, he slams his full length inside me. I give out a sharp moan and realize he never removed his finger from my ass. All thoughts fly from my mind as he pulls out of my cunt and drills back in repeatedly. I'm going to come hard, I can tell. He grabs my ponytail with the hand that doesn't have a finger in my ass, and forces my head up.

I'm looking across the room at the glass enclosure and realize the bearded dragon is staring at me. Mr. Parks rams into my cunt over and over again, while he moves his finger in and out of my ass. The intense emotions are too much, and I continue to lock eyes with the bearded dragon as I peak and come harder than I ever have in my life. I let out a strangled scream that I quickly cut off by clenching my teeth when I realize I can't be screaming in the middle of the day. My pussy walls vibrate and spasm while I shiver and shake with an extended orgasm. Waves of pleasure wash over me, down to my toes.

Mr. Parks groans loudly and jerks against me, pushing his finger a little farther into my ass as he spurts his hot cum inside my aching cave. I close my eyes as I come down from my peak, and when he lets go of my hair, I lay my head down on the desk. He removes his finger and cock from my various holes, and he plops down in his office chair.

He's out of breath and panting. "My god, you are amazing."

His compliment warms my core, but I don't know how much I actually did. I just walked into his office and laid here. He did all the work.

I stand up, a little unsteadily, and he holds his hand out to support me while I get my balance. When he can tell I'm fine, he lets go and pulls out wet wipes from his desk drawer. Do they just keep a stash of them normally, or is this a new thing for me?

He offers the package to me. "Do you want one?"

I contemplate it for a minute before shaking my head. "No, thank you."

I collect my clothes and get dressed again, checking myself in a small mirror on his wall to make sure I'm presentable.

I'm about to leave his office and he stops me.

"Miranda?"

I glance at him, questioning.

"Next time I'm going to try two fingers."

My pussy buzzes at that thought. I smile at him and give him a jaunty salute. "I look forward to it, sir."

I give the bearded dragon one last glance before walking out the door, and I swear it's looking at me in disapproval. Even the bearded dragon knows I'm a slut deep down, which thrills me to my core.

The End

# BONDING WITH THE BOSS

# CHAPTER 1

By the time Friday rolls around, I'm a bit of a mess. This work week has been off-the-charts crazy for me. If someone had told me last week that I was going to have slept with two of my bosses by now, I don't think I would have believed them. The insane part about this is that my husband, Jon, is fully supporting me in this endeavor. How many husbands want their wives to fuck her bosses without asking for some quid pro quo? I'm not the sharing type, and while I'm very secure in myself, I just don't like the idea that Jon could fall in love with someone else. He's the best thing about my life, and I wouldn't sleep around if he hadn't pushed me to do this.

I also know my husband, and he lets Rusty—his pet name for his cock—influence important decisions. Jon and Rusty are an impulsive pair, and they would both fall head over heels for the first curvy brunette that bats her eyelashes at them. Luckily, it's not an issue, and Jon is just incredibly turned on by the thought of me fucking my way through town, as long as I come home and tell him all about it.

I'm still a little wet over what took place with Jon last night after I got fingered by my boss's finger at work. Jon is a smart guy and all, but it's almost as if he never contemplated doing me in the ass before. My story of what transpired at work awoke the beast in him, and now my ass is fair game as far as he's concerned. I guess I'll just say that I had more than one man's finger in my bum yesterday and it was hot.

But all of that with Jon took more time last night than I would have preferred, and I'm exhausted this morning. I considered calling in sick, but that isn't fair to the receptionist, Cindy, when we're the only office staff working right now. The paralegal is out for two weeks on vacation and I can't leave Cindy to fend for herself, especially not when my reason is lack of sleep and being oversexed from fucking my bosses and my husband.

There's only one boss left that I haven't fucked—at least until Monday when the new partner joins the firm. This last boss, Mr. Knight, is the one I have the least amount of contact with. If I'm being honest, he's scary in a sexy way. Because I don't know him well, I've decided he needs to approach me if he wants me. I will not be slipping notes under his door offering my services, like I did for Mr. Parks. Mr. Knight didn't give any indication all week that he was interested in me, so I'm not sure if he's planning on having fun with me or not. I'm half hoping it isn't today. A long weekend of sleep sounds nice before I have another fuck fest with a horny husband when I get off work.

I won't lie. A tiny part of me considered how planned out all of this appears to be. Mr. Jacobs, the senior partner, first has me, and then Mr. Parks was incredibly prepared and inventive with his sexual choices. I wonder if they had a meeting and discussed scheduling of who has me when and what they are planning to do to me? I stifle a yawn at that thought while I pull into the office parking lot. Overall, I'm having a blast, but I may need a break if Jon expects sex every night after I get fucked at work. Twice-daily fucking only sounds good when you have plenty of sleep.

The office is empty when I walk in five minutes late. Cindy isn't at the front desk and the halls are devoid of any lawyers. I plop down in my chair and notice a notecard with my name on it. Guess the moment of truth is upon me. I rip it open and it's a handwritten letter from Mr. Knight.

*Miranda,*

*I want you to take the weekend to relax and be refreshed and prepared for me on Monday. Please come to work fully shaved and wearing pigtails.*

*Sincerely,*

*Mr. Knight*

When I close the card, my brain is a kaleidoscope of thoughts and I'm relieved to have a break today. This agreement wasn't well-planned so I know there will be times in the future I might decline their advances, but I didn't want to do that until we had an established routine.

I contemplate the note again. Fully shaved sounds hot, but what is up with wanting me in pigtails?

I need to get some work done since I've been a bit of a slacker the last two days, but I take a quick second to type a text to my husband to tell him nothing sexual is happening today. I included the info that Mr. Knight wants me shaved and in pigtails on Monday. A few minutes later he texts back, "Can I shave you?" I giggle at the message. That's my goofy husband for you. I reply and tell him that only good boys get to shave me and then set my phone down and attempt to avoid checking for a reply.

I successfully ignore it for a couple of hours until I take a break and see five text messages from Jon, pleading to shave me and saying he'll be the best boy there is. His fifth message is so outrageous. My giggle is louder than I intended. Deciding to put him out of his misery, I tell him I love him and he can shave me. His only response to that is a fire emoji, which I take to be a good sign. He better not be planning this shave party tonight. A nap after work sounds perfect, and I don't want a two-day stubble by Monday.

The rest of my day goes by fast. Before I know it, I'm saying goodbye to Cindy and back in my car. I only saw Mr. Jacobs once, and the other two lawyers were in depositions all day. Mr. Jacobs made small talk with me about weekend plans with zero sexual banter. He treated me like the employee I was before, which was a relief. I don't want to worry about hiding my office flings from Cindy.

# CHAPTER 2

I swear I blink and the next thing I know I'm back in my car Monday morning heading to work. My weekend was a haze of sleeping, relaxing, more wild sex with my husband, and then a hilarious shaving session last night before bed. After shaving me, Jon had to inspect the product thoroughly, which somehow included putting his finger in my ass again. This newly awoken sexual energy in Jon has been the jolt our marriage needed. It was one long, playful weekend, but now that Monday has finally arrived, I'm nervous.

I'm not late to work today since I didn't want the drive-thru coffee stand workers to see my hairstyle. After parking my car, I glance in the rearview mirror and fiddle with my necklace. It's a sterling silver pendant that was a gift from my husband, and spells out the word "kitten," which is the pet name he calls me. I tug the pigtails self-consciously. Even though I know I look cute, I also think I'm too old to wear pigtails to work.

Mr. Knight didn't specify braids, but this is the only way to keep it from being a mess by the end of the day. Unfortunately, I didn't realize how Britney Spears-esque this would all appear in my short black skirt, white button-down shirt, and chunky black shoes. At least I have brown hair instead of blonde like her. Halfway to work it hits me: I'm self-conscious because it seems as if I am trying to be a sexy young kitten at my age. And while it's adorable at home, it doesn't seem work-appropriate.

Deciding it's too late to do anything else, I stroll into the office with a sassy swing in my step and attempt to own the outfit. My bravado lasts all of five seconds until Cindy blinks a wide-eyed stare at me and stammers out a hesitant hello. Giving her a tiny smile, I make a fast dash to my little corner. Thank God the paralegal is off for one more week. The fewer people to observe my shame, the better.

Thinking I can just keep my head down and stay focused on work, I attempt to tune everything out. At one point I glimpse someone out of the corner of my eye and I realize it's the new partner, Mr. Daniels, wandering down the hall away from me. Oh shit, this is his first day at the office. But at least he didn't walk towards me. I pretend to myself that I'm hidden behind a shield of invisibility.

It's also been years since I've completely shaved down below. Usually I do a trim job, but Jon prefers a more natural look, so over time I've become lazy. I forgot how sensitive and feminine it feels when you're hairless. I'm noticing the rub of my silk panties and, coupled with the sexual tension about the unknown with Mr. Knight, I'm turned on and wishing Mr. Knight would find me sooner rather than later.

Mr. Knight doesn't instant message me, or approach me by lunch time. Everyone, other than Mr. Knight, has spotted my outfit by now, so an hour ago I said "fuck it" and strutted around the office as if it was my personal stage and I really was Britney Spears. Mr. Jacobs gave me a sly smile once in passing and I got a bit of a tingle from the appreciative expression in his glance. I wanted to say, "Yeah, you know you want a piece of this," but there's no way in hell I'd state that to my boss. The idea of him bending me over his desk again while

I'm wearing this outfit is extremely appealing. Mr. Jacobs does such a thorough job from behind.

Since I'm not hiding out at my desk any longer, I take my sexy self into the break room and put in some earbuds to rock out to my Britney Spears theme song while I eat a sandwich. My back is to the entrance and I'm jamming along, so I almost fly out of my seat when someone taps me on my shoulder to get my attention.

Mr. Knight is standing behind me with a half-amused, dark, smoldering expression. I do not know what the look in his eye means, but my pussy clenches in response, and I stop chewing and forget to breathe for a second. I fumble to turn off my music so I can see what he wants.

"Miranda, when you're done with lunch, I would like you to come to my office."

I swallow the bite of sandwich in my mouth and stammer out, "Yes, sir."

Mr. Knight doesn't reply and leaves the break room. Exhaling a whoosh of air, I take a moment to appreciate how attractive Mr. Knight is. He might be a tad scary, but that only adds to his appeal. Today he has on a black suit with a blue shirt and tie. He must have had meetings this morning, which would explain why I hadn't seen him yet. He's in his mid-to-late 40s, fit, with a bigger body type and broad shoulders. I'd hazard a guess the coaches hounded him to play football in high school. My pussy gives a nice hum and I'm wet from the encounter. She's obviously all on board with being the cheerleader to his quarterback. I pack up my lunch and wonder if he approves of the braids.

# CHAPTER 3

Mr. Knight's office is in the back corner, so I take the side halls to avoid seeing Cindy. I'm semi-amazed that she hasn't figured out what is going on in the office yet. She's nice, and I don't think she's the type of person who would ever question me, but that doesn't mean she wouldn't be silently judging my harlot soul. I'm hoping to not ruin our working relationship while continuing my fuck fest with the men. I would say we could do it discreetly, but it all depends on how many times they expect me to comply with special requests for hair or clothing. It would be hard to feign innocence if one of them asked me to dress as a slutty nun.

The thought of me being in costume gives me the giggles. I'm nervous when I knock on Mr. Knight's door, which adds to the chuckling. By the time he tells me to come in, I'm practically outright laughing at the mental picture of how stupid I look standing outside his door in this outfit. When I walk in giggling like a loon, the glare he throws my way shuts me up fast. *Oh, no, I made daddy cranky.* One last small giggle escapes at the thought of calling him daddy.

I'm rarely in his office and it's dimmer than the other offices because this back corner of the building doesn't get afternoon sunlight. He's sitting behind his dark cherry wood desk, and he's decorated his office in darker colors. I'm not sure what's come over me today, but my mind immediately wants to laugh over how ridiculous this all is. The dark, handsome, brooding lawyer in his dungeon office who has lured the cute, pigtailed woman in for debauchery. If he expects me to roleplay anything, I'm not sure I could oblige today. I'd just giggle the entire time.

Mr. Knight frowns at me and drums his fingers on his desk. The hollow beat the only sound breaking the silence. I nervously fiddle with my kitten necklace and shiver. Sexual excitement replaces the hilarity of the situation, and I hope he's going to bend me over the desk. I might as well be three for three on being bent over the office desks. Something tells me that Mr. Knight won't be gentle about it and based on how wet I am at the thought, my body doesn't mind.

When he finally speaks, it's toneless, so I can't tell if he's angry at me. "Miranda, remove all your clothes and stand in the middle of the room."

*Oh, shit.* I haven't been completely naked yet with any of them, and the thought is strangely erotic. I mean, I've had two other cocks inside of me, but being exposed is more personal somehow. Instead of responding, I kick off my shoes and they clatter across the room. As I'm unzipping my skirt and unbuttoning my top, Mr. Knight opens a drawer and removes some items that he lays out on the top of the desk.

I don't pay him much mind because my hands are shaking and it's almost impossible to get my shirt unbuttoned. When I finally free the buttons, I drop my shirt to the floor, along with my skirt. I'm standing in a pair of white satin panties and matching bra when my attention focuses on the items sitting on the desk. He's laid out a bundle of rope and oddly angled scissors I would expect to see at a doctor's office. *Uh, what the shit?* I freeze and stare at Mr. Knight with wide eyes.

Mr. Knight leans back in his chair and matter-of-factly states, "Miranda, you have two options. Option A is, I bend you over my desk and fuck you so hard your head spins."

He pauses for a moment to let that sink in, and my pussy hums in approval. I might get bent over this third desk after all. I'm internally doing a happy dance and about ready to blurt out that I want option A, but he continues.

"Option B is, I bind your ankles together, lay you on your back on the desk, and shove your knees to your chest while I fuck you. Then each time I call you to my office, I will tie you up differently."

My brain blips out while I imagine that possibility. An intense yearning hits me like a truck. I've always secretly thrilled over the idea of being bound, but my husband is goofy and playful, so it wasn't really something I would ask for. I never considered this hotwife deal would include the possibility of me being able to live out my sexual fantasies. Being bent over all the surfaces in the office by a bunch of sexy lawyers was as far as my mind got.

Mr. Knight's steely voice penetrates my sexual haze. "So, Miranda, which will it be?"

I'm visibly shaking when I whisper my reply. "Option B, please."

Mr. Knight stands up and walks around the desk, bringing the rope and the odd scissors with him.

"Finish undressing and sit on the edge of the desk."

I quickly drop my panties to the floor and unhook my bra. The hard surface is cold against my bare ass as Mr. Knight kneels in front of me and pulls my feet together, and I watch fascinated as he deftly folds the piece of rope in half and wraps it around my ankles, looping one piece through the other to create tension.

As he loops the rope around my calves, he talks soothingly to me. "If at any point you want released, use the word 'red' and I will immediately stop and free you. Do you understand?" He pauses and looks up at me.

*Oh, I guess that's what the scissors are for.* I'm still wide-eyed and crazy turned on, but nod yes, but that doesn't seem to please him.

"Say the word if you understand."

I shiver before replying. "Red."

He nods satisfied and continues wrapping my ankles. "Do you have any medical conditions I need to know about?"

*Uh, what?* This is not the way I expected this conversation to go, but him being careful with me is even more of a turn-on than I thought possible. I squirm from the buzz he's creating in my pussy, and my voice is firm when I reply, "No".

Satisfied that I'm secure, he pulls the tail of the rope through the beginning loop he made, and finishes it by wrapping the tail between my ankles and creating some complex hoop and loop thing to secure everything. He talks me through everything he's doing and as he winds the rope, I shake from need and excitement. I don't really understand everything he did, but the result is that my ankles are bound in such a way that there's no possibility of getting loose without help. He takes a moment to test that the rope isn't so binding that it would cut off circulation. When he's assured, he stands up and steps back to admire me.

My wrists are free, so I'm not expecting the ripple of vulnerability that pulsates through my mind. This isn't scary and I'm so wet his desk might require a cleaning when we're done, but knowing that he could do whatever he wanted with me and it would be tougher for me to fight him off is hard to not acknowledge. I'm breathless, aching, and I consented to this, so I'm totally down with everything that's happening. The conflicting emotions just momentarily surprise me.

Mr. Knight walks behind me and removes the few personal items he had scattered on his desk. It's just me and his closed laptop on the surface now. I peek at him over my shoulder as he strips out of his suit. A thrill runs through me when I realize he's disrobing fully as well. This is not some quickie fuck in his office. This is a full-blown encounter, and I'm doubly thankful that Cindy didn't see me come in here.

Once he's naked, he comes around to stand in front of me. He's muscular, but his clothes hid a tiny belly which is super sexy on him. He's rocking the hot dad bod and I want to run my hands over his chest and stomach but hold back. I'm not sure if that's allowed. He's fully erect, and his cock brushes against my knees. I'm looking up at him, ready for him to push me down and take me, but he fingers the sterling silver kitten necklace. He traces the outline of the word against my skin, and I shiver.

His voice is soft and husky when he asks, "So you're Kitten?"

I simply answer, "Yes."

For the first time today, he smiles at me as he presses me back on the desk and I shiver when my skin makes contact with the cool surface.

"Well, Kitten, are you ready to be fucked?"

I don't answer him since it seems to not require one. Hearing my husband's pet name come out of his mouth is hot in a forbidden way, and I gasp as he lifts my legs to press my knees to my chest. He literally climbs up onto the desk with me, and I silently wish there was a mirror in his office. I bet we look amazing.

I expect him to shove into me and get right to it, but he fingers me for a moment to make sure I'm wet and turned on. The entire time he was tying the rope was one long session of foreplay, so I'm more than ready to be fucked. I moan softly as he nudges his rod against my slippery folds and slides in. My cave walls stretch and mold around him, but he doesn't give me much time to adjust before he pulls out and thrusts back in, setting a pace that is almost like a jackhammer.

He's not as thick as Mr. Jacobs, but I'm not complaining. He's hitting all the right spots, and I'm panting and pushing against him with every lunge. Oh, shit, this is completely amazing. I grip the sides of the desk with my hands and give a tiny squeal each time he bottoms out as deep as he can go. Knowing I can't separate my ankles and may get tied up in more inventive ways in the future is driving me towards my orgasm.

I'm repeatedly chanting "Oh my God," which is my signature Miranda mode that means whatever is happening is beyond awesome, and the pleasure is mounting in my core. Each nudge against my entrance is a tiny shudder closer to the edge. Mr. Knight adjusts positions slightly, and he pushes my legs a little closer to my chest.

The shift pulls me over the crest. He's hitting different nerve endings and I explode. My entire body shakes as waves of pleasure sweep me to a higher plane of existence. I almost have an out-of-body experience where my bliss is so great that I visualize myself lying on the desk, convulsing as I come harder than I have ever come in my life, while I scream out long and loud. I don't hold back vocally, and I'm beyond caring.

During the longest orgasm in my 28 years, a part of my brain recognizes that Mr. Knight also peaks. He groans loudly and thrusts against me roughly as he shudders, spurting his load of hot cum, coating my inner walls. As I come down from my climax, I notice the position I am in has become uncomfortable with his weight against me. Before I can ask to lower my legs, he shifts off me and helps me slowly unbend.

He climbs off the desk while I lay there in a daze. My brain still isn't working fully and I'm relaxed and content to not move.

When I'm silent, he seems concerned. "Are you okay?"

My voice is thick and slightly hoarse. "Uh... yes."

In my haze, I watch him go to a mini fridge and pull out a bottle of water, open it, and bring it over to me. He helps me prop myself up on my elbows to take a sip. The crisp, cool water flowing down my throat snaps me out of my stupor.

I giggle softly. "I think you almost fucked my brains out."

He moves to my ankles and starts undoing the rope, but a satisfied smile blossoms on his face.

"I aim to please," is his only reply.

When he's done removing the rope, he massages my ankles and gently flexes them to make sure nothing hurts. Everything feels fine, so I stretch my legs and toes at him and wiggle them to prove it. He captures my feet and kisses the tops of them before moving around to the back of his desk to put his suit on. I gently swing my legs over the side and sit up slowly. I'm physically fine, but mentally I'm still shaking.

This experience was more than I was expecting, and it's going to take longer to process than just a few moments sitting in his office. I'm slightly scared at how hard I came, and I'm not sure how detailed to get with my husband. I also know I don't want to stop with Mr. Knight, and if I tell Jon exactly how this is affecting me, he might have issues with it continuing.

I'm battling my internal demons when Mr. Knight comes around the desk, mostly clothed, and tips my chin up, forcing me to glance up at him. He gently asks, "are you doing okay?"

I try to nod my head, but I feel close to tears. I don't know how to explain to him he just gave me the best sex of my life and it scares me. While I'm trying to figure out how to articulate something, he wraps his arms around me and rubs my back. I'm shocked by the gesture, but gratefully lean into him. His office smells like sex now, but his clothes have a pleasant sandalwood scent. I inhale deeply and some of my angst drains away.

He murmurs, "How did that go for you?" He still seems worried, and I want to assure him I'm fine. The longer he hugs me and rubs my back, the more that is true.

I choose to be honest. "I wasn't expecting it to be so fabulous."

Mr. Knight gives a small snort, and I hope I didn't just stroke his ego up another notch. It doesn't seem like he needs much help in that department.

When he steps back from hugging me, he grins and his blue eyes sparkle. "Don't decide now, but if you want to explore more of this, I know plenty more delightful ways to tie you up."

I consider telling him I don't need to think about it and I'm all in, but realize there is some wisdom in his plan. Before I decide, I should see how Jon reacts tonight when I tell him about this encounter.

Mr. Knight brings my clothes over to me, and when I stand up, he helps me get dressed. He tugs on my braids a little sheepishly, "I had plans for these pigtails but got distracted." Before I can respond, he shrugs. "Maybe next time."

Thinking of a possible next time thrills me. I want more of this than I've ever wanted anything. Before I leave his office, I give my clothes one final adjustment and run my fingers across my kitten necklace to make sure it's laying flat. In that moment I make a snap decision to not tell Jon that Mr. Knight called me Kitten.

The End

# BREAKING IN THE JUNIOR PARTNER

# CHAPTER 1

As I drive to work on Tuesday, Mr. Knight consumes my thoughts. I'm still shaken from my experience with him at work yesterday. He'd brought me into his office and given me the choice of being bent over his desk or lying on my back with my ankles bound while he fucked me. I chose the tied-up option, thinking I would get an interesting new adventure, but it ended up being more intense than I imagined. Not only was the sex fabulous, but the tender way he treated me afterwards elevated it beyond just a hot office fuck. My emotions are unsettled, and I don't know what to think. I didn't expect to be ravished and then cared for. After our trysts, none of the other lawyers did anything but bid me goodbye.

Last night was awkward at home with my husband, Jon. I explained what happened, but when he got super horny and tried to paw me, I lied and said I was too tired and not in the mood. In reality, Jon couldn't give me what I needed. Jon spent last evening researching bondage and jacking off. Now he thinks he's going to become a binding master and rock my world. The idea intrigues me and I won't discourage him, but part of the thrill with Mr. Knight was his aura of power. I'm not sure my goofy husband could pull that off. But maybe once he has me bound and at his mercy? I don't know. At the moment, I can't see it.

I spent the evening replaying in my head every minute detail of what Mr. Knight had done to me, and I ached to experience it again. I even had a dream that night where Mr. Knight handcuffed my wrists together and used a hook on a wall above me to restrain me. He stimulated every inch of my body, me totally at his mercy while I squirmed and moaned. I orgasmed in my dream, which isn't common at all. I can count on one hand the times I remember climaxing while asleep. Usually I'm almost there and wake up, or the dream is just sexual frustration and edging. Because of this, I woke up with a wet and throbbing pussy.

So these factors are rattling in my head as I stroll into the office building. I wave good morning to the receptionist, Cindy, but I don't stop to chat. I'm afraid of running into Mr. Knight. If he ignores me like he used to, it might hurt. Emotionally, I want yesterday to have meant something to him because it sure as heck had meaning for me, but intellectually I know it shouldn't. Even if my husband learns how to tie me up and we add in some kinky bedroom stuff, Mr. Knight is always going to have that spot in my mind as the first person to give me pleasure so intense that it scared me. But If he's just a douchebag who doesn't speak to me ever again, does he deserve that distinction?

And then there's the matter of Mr. Knight's offer to tie me up in different ways. Hoping to keep that detail to myself, I purposely didn't mention it to Jon. Now that Jon wants to experiment with his newfound interest, I need to talk to him. He might request I stop with Mr. Knight for now. I'd like to say I would abide by my husband's wishes, but I know deep down that in the moment, if Mr. Knight pulled out some rope, I would say "please, and thank you, Sir,"

I'm not in the best headspace and uncertain what to expect, yet again, from my bosses this week. The new lawyer, Mr. Daniels, started yesterday, and I have slight anxiety over him as well. Surely they won't ask me to fuck the new guy, right? It's not like I knew the rest of them that well, but I'd worked with them for a while and we had some sort of rapport. Is Mr. Daniels going to walk up to me and demand I bend over for him also? That might be a tad awkward.

My pussy buzzes at the thought and I smirk at myself. My beaver is a slut, and she can't help it. Pretty sure she'd be willing to get pegged by the hobo who sleeps behind Home Depot if I let her have free rein over my actions. I giggle a little at the hobo idea. I don't know if hobo is a politically correct word, but owning a house means we're at Home Depot often, so I see the man fairly regularly. If he showered and put on clean clothes, I'm certain he'd be hella hot. He has that rangy body that gives him a hungry appearance, like he'd force you to your knees and face fuck you while you writhe in pleasure. I squirm in my chair a little. Between my dream and now thinking of Mr. Hot Hobo, I'm more than slightly wet.

# CHAPTER 2

I'm daydreaming about the hobo when I notice my interoffice instant messenger flashing. It's the senior partner, Mr. Jacobs, requesting my presence in his office. Uh... oh shit. Is he going to sex me up? I instantly drench my panties and I'm shaking as I walk to his office. Mr. Jacobs is comfortable and safe, so I allow the excitement to build. I know what to expect from him. He likes me bent over his desk, and my twat is obviously down for that.

A voice in my head tells me I'd prefer being tied up and fucked by Mr. Knight, and I try to push the thought away. That wasn't the bargain, and Mr. Jacobs may demand his turn with me. And Mr. Parks promised to stick more fingers up my ass. He's training me for full anal, and I still crave that experience as well. A tiny whisper in my brain says I'd give that all up to fuck Mr. Knight again.

Silently cursing myself, I push the thought aside as I knock on Mr. Jacobs's office door.

"Come in."

My long brown hair is in one braid that falls forward over my shoulder as I am getting my lunch and purse out of the car. As I walk in, I toss the braid back over my shoulder and imagine Mr. Jacobs tugging on it while fucking me from behind. I'm getting more on board with the idea of being with Mr. Jacobs again, so when he tells me to sit down, I freeze. *What? He wants to talk?*

I perch on the edge of the chair and cross my ankles. I've taken to wearing loose skirts in case I get bent over various locations, so I smooth down the black fabric and attempt to appear demure. If he wants to negotiate terms, I have some things I want to say.

Mr. Jacobs starts out with a fatherly tone. "Miranda, we have a problem."

I'm shocked and pause awkwardly for a few seconds. Since I wasn't expecting this, my eyes grow big and I stutter, "A pro...bb...blem?"

I wince a little at my ineptitude. *Smooth move there, Miranda.*

Mr. Jacobs taps a pen against the desktop and my pounding heart mirrors the clicking beats against the wood. Yep, I'm about to get fired. This happens when you fuck the bosses and they finish with you. Tears sting behind my eyes and I grip the chair arms to hide my trembling hands. Jon is going to be so pissed.

Mr. Jacobs sighs and stops tapping the pen before continuing. "Mr. Daniels doesn't believe you will fuck him and thinks we're trying to fire him by making him the subject of a sexual harassment lawsuit."

*Uh... What?* I haven't seen Mr. Daniels yet today, but yesterday he was looking quite yummy with his rich, warm brown skin and sexy grin. If I hadn't been so embarrassed to be dressed up like an aging Britney Spears with pigtails, I might have appreciated running into Mr. Daniels more often. The brief times I saw him, he always had a smile and a twinkle in his eyes, so he seemed jovial and not intimidating in the slightest.

Realizing that Mr. Jacobs expects me to respond, I cough a little to clear my throat. "I think it's a reasonable concern. If I wasn't the woman doing this, I would feel the same way."

I don't add that I already fear for my job since I thought he was about to fire me when he said there was a problem. I'll just keep that tidbit of information to myself.

"I need you to seduce him."

I giggle at Mr. Jacobs's announcement, assuming he's joking. "Yeah, not happening."

Does my boss know me at all? I'm adorable, but awkward as fuck and me trying to entice someone intentionally is a joke. My best pickup line is, "Are you related to Yoda? Cuz Yoda-licious!" It doesn't go down as well as one would assume, even with the geeky crowd.

Mr. Jacobs doesn't look amused, and his voice is stern. "I'm not kidding, Miranda."

Oh, shit. I angered Daddy. I sober up and shelve my jokester attitude, muttering, "I don't think I can do it."

"I want to offer you a deal."

My pussy perks up at the offer. *Ooooh, please be sexual!* I tell her to calm the fuck down and the compromise will probably be he won't fire my ass if I do it.

"If you seduce Mr. Daniels tomorrow, on Friday after work we'll all stay late for a party."

I tip my head, confused. "A party?"

"Yes. The four of us will take turns fucking you on the conference room table."

I pause and think of how to respond. Jon and I still haven't talked about multiple partners at once, plus I'm uncertain I want to do this. I have to seduce the new guy tomorrow and service four guys on Friday? This seems more like a party for them than it does for me.

I don't want to hint that his offer stinks, and search for another way out. "I need to speak to my husband first."

Mr. Jacobs leans back and crosses his hands, resting them on his stomach. "Sure, and when you talk to him, tell him he's welcome to watch over Zoom. We can connect him to the conference room cameras."

A jolt of sexual energy buzzes through me when he mentions streaming me. Now *THAT* makes the offer interesting. I don't know if Jon would want to watch, but it's worth considering.

Mr. Jacobs stands, signaling the meeting is over. "Talk to your husband tonight. If he agrees, come to work tomorrow and seduce Mr. Daniels."

I stand up, mumble an okay, and walk out of his room like a zombie. My brain is running in 20 million directions at once. Do I want to do this? Will Jon even let me, and will he be interested in watching? So many unanswered questions.

I'm not paying attention to my surroundings, and when I turn the corner to get to my desk, Mr. Knight is standing next to it and I stumble and trip. I don't fall all the way to the floor because he catches me and helps me stand up.

"Are you okay?" He has a concerned expression, and it warms me. He isn't ignoring me!

"I'm fine, just distracted."

Mr. Knight assesses me critically and, deeming me fine, gestures towards my desk. "I was leaving you something. Let me know what you think?"

I shoot a glance at my desk as he walks away. There is a purple bag resting in the center and my heart jumps into my throat. *Oh my God. He brought me a gift?* I sit down and dig into the bag. On top is a notecard, which I set aside, and right below that is a compact bundle of the same rope he tied me up in.

My brain freezes for a good five seconds as I stare at the rope before a rush of emotion and sexual energy almost overwhelms me. Jesus Christ! I visualize the moment in his office where he's got me on my back with my ankles bound, and he's shoving my knees to my chest and entering me. My pussy clenches and if I had been edging today, I might have just orgasmed. I'm wetter than I was earlier, and my hands are shaking when I pick up the note.

*Miranda,*

*I want to add in another offer for the office party. If you are interested, I could restrain you however you desire and we'd fuck you like that. If you need to think it over, message me before Friday and let me know.*

*Mr. Knight.*

My brain sputters. *YES, A THOUSAND TIMES, YES!* I need to go home to Jon and talk to him, but it's not even lunchtime. UGH! I can't believe he fucking wants to restrain me in the conference room. This is so unbelievably hot. I wiggle in my chair, rubbing my pussy against the seat, but it's not helping matters. I glance around to make sure no one is watching, get up, and scamper to the restroom.

I close the door behind me and lock it. Luckily, it's a one-person bathroom. I lean against the wall and pull my skirt up with one hand and furiously rub my pussy through my wet panties with the other hand. My legs tremble and I slide down the wall until my butt touches the ground. My skirt is pulled up and my legs splayed out wide, knees bent and my high heels flat on the ground. The position gives me the access to my cave of wonders that I require, though I probably look like a crazy woman. I shove my panties aside and slip my fingers between my slick folds, moaning in pleasure as I furiously massage my clit in small circles.

I thrust a finger inside and imagine it's Mr. Knight for a moment before moving back to focus all my attention on my clit. I'm rubbing faster and moaning, and I'm being loud, but I don't give a damn.

The orgasm hits me hard and I groan as my thighs shake and waves of pleasure radiate from my core.

As I come down from the bliss, I relax and giggle. That might have been the fastest I've ever gone from zero to sixty with an orgasm. Though I was probably already at a ten or twenty and not starting at zero. But it still was impressively fast.

I stagger off the floor, using the wall as leverage, and wash my hands and straighten my clothes. When I open the bathroom door, my cheeks are a bright red and I peek around, hoping no one is close by. I breathe a sigh of relief when I don't see anyone as I slink back to my desk.

I'm relaxed after my orgasm, though still slightly turned on whenever I glance at the bag containing the rope. Mr. Knight sure knows how to make my head spin. I'm eager to get home to Jon, and the day drags on forever. This question deserves a face-to-face conversation, and I decide not to text the question to my husband.

When it's finally quitting time, I hurry out after saying goodnight to Cindy. I glance in the rearview mirror before starting the car and my blue eyes are clear, bright, and excited. It's going to be a long wait until Jon gets home.

# CHAPTER 3

The next morning, I yawn and stumble around, groggy as all heck from the previous night. You could say that Jon was all on board this party plan, and he enthusiastically fucked me while telling me exactly how hot the idea of watching me fuck my bosses through Zoom made him. I showed him the rope that Mr. Knight gave me, and he stole it and stashed it away somewhere. I hope Mr. Knight didn't need that back. Jon was so eager and thrilled when I handed it to him. I can only imagine he'll be masturbating and grinding the rope all over his cock as soon as I walk out the door. He leaves for work later than I do, and I assume his morning routine includes rubbing one out once I'm gone. He jokes that an orgasm focuses him, but I'm pretty sure he's just looking for excuses.

I'm feeling refreshed after my shower and I choose my outfit carefully. If I have to seduce Mr. Daniels, I better play the part well. Smoothing a pair of black thigh-high stockings up my legs, I slip on another black skirt and white button-down shirt. I have entirely too many black skirts, but it's my standard uniform for work since they go with every blouse I own. Wedge platform shoes complete my look. I want to be sexy, but not kill myself walking around on stilts all day.

Deciding today it would not be good to be late to work, I skip the espresso stand. I'll drink the coffee at the office like a peasant. I sigh as I pull into my parking spot at the office. It's only Wednesday and I have zero clue how I'm going to seduce Mr. Daniels, and I wish this day was over already. I want to focus all my excitement on Friday and can't wait for the end of the week to arrive.

Cindy isn't at the front desk when I arrive, so I settle in at my station seeing no one. I'm slightly nauseated whenever I wonder how to approach Mr. Daniels. I decide to ignore the problem and concentrate on my morning routine until I notice my instant messenger flash at me. Oh, shit. What now? When I see Mr. Daniels's icon flashing, I freak out and close my eyes to count to ten, breathing deeply to relax myself. This is probably work-related and nothing to get my panties in a bunch about.

When I'm feeling calmer, I open the message.

`"Hey. Mr. Jacobs said you need to talk to me this morning. What can I do for you?"`

Ooooh, that sneaky bastard. He's forcing my hand. My stomach instantly ties up into knots again. What in the hell do I even say? I could opt for the blunt approach and just be like, "Hey, want to fuck?" I blush when I imagine typing that out and know that isn't something I can do. My fingers are shaking when I finally decide.

`"Yes. Mr. Jacobs said you were skeptical about my arrangement with them, and I wanted to assure you I am a willing participant."`

When I press send, I squeal quietly. Oh my God. How will he respond? I'm hoping he takes the lead from this point. I advised him I'm down with it. Maybe he'll tell me to come to his office for some afternoon delight?

He's typing and I'm anxious as I see the little dots flash for longer than they should if he was only telling to come fuck him.

"I'm sorry, but I don't believe this and I
can't afford to lose my job."

Oh, shit. My vision of a conference room fuck fest crumbles. This
can't happen! Before I lose the nerve, I stand up and march down
the hall to Mr. Daniels's office. I rap on the door and wait for him to
tell me to enter. As soon as I step into the room, I'm breathless and
uncertain what to say.

I glance around, looking for anything for inspiration. On his desk
is one of the company-issued packages of moist towelettes that all the
lawyers now seem to stash in their rooms to clean themselves up with
after fucking me. I have the insane urge to giggle, but I know that
wouldn't go over well at this moment.

Mr. Daniels sits in his office chair, frozen, and staring at me. Even
when he's uncomfortable, he's still gorgeous. I love the warm brown
of his skin, and today he's wearing black trousers with a light blue
shirt. He must not have any depositions today because he's missing
a suit jacket and tie, and the top few buttons of his shirt are open.
When he sees me glance at the moist towelettes, he shifts uncomfort-
ably in his seat.

"Uh, Mr. Jacobs just dropped those off."

Seeing how adorably distressed he appears gives me courage. I push
off from the door and sashay towards him, putting an extra swing to
my hips. Thank God I opted for the chunky heels. I pause by his desk
and lean my hip on the edge while raising a knee to force my skirt up.
I couldn't have planned the outfit better. The skirt rides up just high
enough to flash the lace top of my thigh-highs.

I arch an eyebrow at him and when I catch him glance down at my
leg, it gives me extra courage. He swallows nervously and fiddles with
his collar. This man is so dang adorable, and I want to soothe him
and then fuck his brains out.

He stumbles over his words. "Miranda, what can I do for you?"

His hesitation makes me braver than I've ever been in my life. I purr at him. "I think you know."

"I can't lose this job." Mr. Daniels looks pained, as if he's uncertain about his answer.

If I don't somehow convince him, my party won't happen. There is no way the firm would risk a lawsuit if Mr. Daniels turned all of us in for sexual harassment. How do I get it across that they won't fire him and that I want to fuck him? He's super sexy and I'm itching to see if his skin is as soft as it appears.

Something on a shelf behind him catches my eye. Mr. Daniels has only been here for a few days, but it looks as if he's brought some trinkets from home with him. Well, well, well, Mr. Daniels is a Star Wars fan. Rebel Alliance member action figures grace the shelf behind his head, and the ghost of a smile flickers across my face. I should have led with my Yoda pickup line. He also has a green lightsaber, the inexpensive kind that doesn't retract. It's just a long green tube that lights up with the click of the button.

Mr. Daniels is still watching me intently, and I slide my hands down my leg and unbuckle my shoe. It drops to the floor with a thud, and I stand up and bend over to remove the other one. I take the last couple of steps towards him in my stocking feet. He's still not saying anything, so I lean over him to get to the shelf behind him. He doesn't move, and I'm not tall, so to reach I have to put my bosom into his face.

As I stretch over him, I hear him take a sharp breath and a pleasant woodsy cologne washes over me. I could close my eyes and pretend I'm seducing him in a forest. I grab a Princess Leia toy and lean back a little to look down at him.

"So which movie is your favorite?"

The figurines are models from the original three movies, so I can guess what he's going to say.

His voice is gruff when he answers. "The Empire Strikes Back."

I smile to myself since his answer didn't disappoint. I play with Princess Leia a moment before reaching across him to return her to the shelf. This time I press my breasts right up against his face and he grabs my waist. I've never been this aggressive before, but his hesitation is turning me on. The longer I'm around him, the more I want to fuck him senseless. I can't decipher whether he's shy or simply scared, but it's hot. That he's not pushing me away from him tells me he's not immune to my charms.

Putting the figurine back, I move aside from him again. He exhales, as if he were holding his breath, and his hands drop from my waist. I keep eye contact with him as I unzip my skirt and unclasp it, letting it fall to the ground and pool at my feet. I'm standing in front of him in a pair of black satin panties, my white button-down shirt, and my black thigh-highs. He can't help but glance down at my legs.

My pussy is wet and tingling. I'm still not exactly sure how to get him to fuck me, but he's not telling me to leave. I glance at his trousers and notice a hardening bulge and flush with the awareness that my sluttiness turns him on. Intending to tease him a little, I turn around and bend over the front of his desk, wiggling my ass as I reach back and push my panties down. I step out of them and look over my shoulder at him, daring him to touch me.

When I feel his hand caress my ass cheek, I shiver. *Oh shit, I think he's going for it!* My heart jumps into my throat and the conference room party is one more step closer.

I expect him to continue caressing me and take over, but after a few rubs, he drops his hand. *Jesus Christ. What's a girl got to do around here to get fucked?*

I stand up, turn, and lean my bare ass on the desk. We're still not talking and mostly just communicating with looks. Guess he needs to see everything. I slowly unbutton my shirt and push it off my shoulders, exposing my white lace bra. The bulge in his trousers has grown larger and I see him flex his hand, as if he wants to touch me. Since he doesn't, I reach behind my back and unhook my bra, letting it fall gracefully down my arms and dropping it on the floor. I didn't intend to take the stockings off, and I'm naked otherwise.

I'm almost out of options and thoughts on what to do. I didn't expect to be basically fully naked without him taking over. What in the hell do I do now? He's breathing deeply, and I consider just pouncing on him. What would he do if I kissed him?

I'm about to try it when I get another idea. I'm leaning on the side of the desk, so I lift a stocking foot and slide it into his crotch. He shifts and spreads his legs to allow me better access, and that is the moment I know I've won. I flush with excitement and become wetter. My legs are open to his gaze, and he's no longer looking me in the eye. I reach a hand to my apex, rubbing my wet folds, and moan.

He shuffles in his chair again, forcing my foot against his hardness. I flex my toes gently as I rub circles around my clit and arch my back. This is a Miranda I have never seen before, and I'm glorying in the sexual freedom while I massage my pussy lips and bean. I close my eyes for a moment and just enjoy the experience while I press my foot against his cock.

When I open my eyes again, I look at his Star Wars figures and lightsaber on the shelves and it gives me an awesome idea. I don't want to get him off with my foot. I want him inside of me. But at the rate he's going, I fear it's not going to happen. He seems content to sit there, letting me caress him with my foot while I bring myself to orgasm. I need to prod him further.

I push off from the desk and slide my foot down on the chair between his thighs, not touching him or hurting him, but I balance on one leg as I reach behind him for the lightsaber. While I grab it,

I make sure my breasts touch his face. I'm hopeful this will prompt him to grab them or my closeness will spur him to fuck me.

He does neither, and my pussy clenches in frustration and need. I lean back until I'm perched on the desk again with the lightsaber in my hands, and I slide my foot against his stiff member again. I touch the lightsaber to his chest and tap him playfully.

Deciding the direct approach might work better, I question him. "Do you want to fuck me?"

There is an immediate change in his demeanor. His dark eyes gleam and he smiles, flashing those beautiful white teeth at me while he mischievously responds. "Maybe."

*Ooooh, so this is how it's going to be?* I smirk at him and reach a hand behind me to grab the moist towelette package. He's obviously puzzled as I open it and remove a wipe. His eyes widen as I clean the end of the light saber with it. I toss the towelette on the floor and lean back slightly on the desk. He watches with disbelief as I bring the tip of the light saber between my legs and force it against my pussy.

I can't believe what I'm about to do, but he's still not moving and I'm so turned on and desperate for something inside of me that anything will do. I moan as I press the lightsaber into my wet hole, and I flex my foot against him as I fuck myself with the toy.

This is the sluttiest thing I've done in my life and I can't believe what I'm doing, but the relief of thrusting the lightsaber in and out of my snatch urges me to continue. I'm distracted when I hear a belt buckle and my pussy clenches in triumph when I see him opening his trousers.

He lifts my foot up and holds on to it as he stands up, letting his trousers fall to his ankles. He's between my legs, holding one foot and standing out of the way of the long toy. His freed joystick swells and pulsates. He's larger than I'm used to, and suddenly the thin lightsaber seems like a joke. I want that monster inside of me. As far as men go, his cock is the most magnificent one I've ever seen. The tip is wide and the veins pop out along the shaft. If I wasn't sitting here with a lightsaber in my cooch, my mouth would be all over him.

Mr. Daniels lets my foot fall gently, and he presses on my shoulder, forcing me to lie back on the desk. I feel various office desk items poke me in my side and torso, but I'm behind caring. When he takes control of the lightsaber and gently nudges it in and out of my pussy, I moan and thrash.

It doesn't take long before he removes it. He drops it and it clammers to the floor; the plastic making a hollow thunk as it hits the side of the desk on its way down. Mr. Daniels hooks his hands underneath my thighs and pulls me more towards the edge so he can sink his cock into me. As his thick tip nudges my tight hole, seeking entrance, I open my legs as wide as possible. I groan loudly as he plunges straight to my core.

"Oh, my God." I moan and pant as he picks up speed. His thickness massages every hidden fold as my walls stretch and shift to accommodate his size. He leans a hand on the desk next to me as he thrusts repeatedly, grunting and moaning along with me. I writhe against him and he's fucking me so hard he's scooting me around. I attempt to grab ahold of something to stabilize my movement, but the only thing I encounter is his hand, so I clutch onto it. He squeezes my hand in response.

I'm going to come soon, and I can feel the pleasure mounting. Mr. Daniels releases my hand and pins both my wrists to the desk while leaning over me further. I glance down at one hand and the contrast of his dark skin and my pale arm is beautiful as tendrils of rapture coil through my body. He drills against me, and I wrap my stocking-covered legs around his hips.

I chant for him to fuck me harder, and he complies, whacking against me as hard as he can. The pressure on my wrists reminds me of being tied up, and as soon as that thought pops into my head, I explode. I scream and convulse against him. Waves of bliss wash over me as I ride the wave of my orgasm. I shudder and my pussy clenches around his cock. With a final swift stroke, his entire body spasms and jerks as I feel spurt after spurt of hot cum filling me up.

I let out a soft giggle as I relax and drop my legs from around his waist. Mr. Daniels leans over and kisses my stomach as he releases my wrists. He straightens up and his cock slips out of me as he sits down in the office chair with a groan.

He sighs and laughs. "You're crazy and amazing."

I prop myself up on my elbows, and he brings my feet together and rubs on them, enjoying the silky fabric. He kisses the tops of my feet and then stands to help me sit up fully.

"Ouch!" I reach for whatever is jabbing me in the back and realize I'm sweaty and there are several pieces of paper sticking to me, and god knows what else.

Mr. Daniels laughs and reaches behind me to pull everything off. When he's satisfied nothing else is sticking to me, he pauses and caresses my cheek before leaning down to kiss me gently. I wasn't expecting that and his lips are strong and sexy, as he takes control and deepens the kiss.

I feel a slight twinge in my nether regions, as if my cooch is trying to revive herself, but I'm also a little sore so I mentally chide her to slow her roll as he breaks off the kiss. Grabbing his hand before he can back away, I twine my fingers through his, enjoying the light and dark contrast again. I wish we were both naked so I could lie against him and enjoy the sight, but we're way beyond that point.

Mr. Daniels helps me off the desk and as I'm getting dressed, he laughs. I glance over at him to see what amuses him, and he's looking at his destroyed desktop. I giggle with him, and as he picks up the lightsaber from the floor, he smirks at me.

"Miranda, I don't think I'm ever going to look at this thing the same way."

I'm almost fully dressed and buckling my shoes, and as I straighten up, I laugh with him. "My husband has a similar one at home, and I don't think I'm ever going to look at it the same either."

Deciding I should probably get back to work before Cindy comes looking for me, I pause in the doorway and give him a sassy smile. "By the way, did they tell you there's a party in the conference room after work on Friday?"

The End

# MIRANDA'S REWARD

# CHAPTER 1

Words cannot describe how eager I am for work on Thursday. I left my house too early and had to stop to get a latte, impatient when the line was long despite knowing it's for the best. Cindy will find it suspicious if I'm early and in a good mood. I can be one or the other, but never both at the same time. Unless it's Friday. That's the only day of the week that happiness is acceptable.

The attorney's office I'm employed at has four lawyers, and they offered me a "party" after work on Friday in the conference room. They're all going to fuck me, and I had to decide if I wanted to be tied up or not. Mr. Knight is the lawyer into bondage, and today I have to give him my answer. The senior partner, Mr. Jacobs, offered to allow my husband, Jon, to watch over Zoom, and Jon is especially eager to see Mr. Knight tie me up so he can see how it's done by someone who knows what he's doing. He's giddy thinking that Mr. Knight might be a master at it. I have nothing to compare it to, so I have no clue. But I'm wet just thinking about it, so I know I want it.

I prance through the double glass doors leading into work, wearing a sexy, bright red flared short skirt, a black button-down shirt, and black ballet flats for a change of pace. My long brown hair is down with minimal styling, which I might regret by the end of the day, but

I have a hair clip in my desk if it gets too messy. I am a woman on a mission, and I need to tell Mr. Knight that I choose the option to be tied up for our party tomorrow in the conference room.

Intending to breeze past Cindy at the front desk so I can hurry and log into my computer to instant message Mr. Knight my request, I pause instead.

"Hey, Cindy. Is Mr. Knight here yet?" I attempt to sound casual, but Cindy's sharp glance proves I failed.

"Yep, I saw him come in a bit ago."

I thank her and scurry to my office area, dropping my purse and water bottle on the surface with a clatter, and set my coffee down. Cindy must sense something by now, right? The thought that she might know how slutty I am thrills me to my core. I love the rush I get from having a secret everyone knows but isn't speaking about, and no one confirms it. When I switch my computer on, inspiration strikes. Fuck instant messenger. I'm going to tell him in person.

Before I lose my nerve, I march to his dark dungeon office in the back corner. Remembering the last time I was in his office, a shiver of delight runs down my spine when I knock on the door. I almost chicken out when he sounds irritable as he calls out for me to come in. I could run to my desk to hide and pretend it wasn't me. But then if I tried to instant messenger him soon about being tied up, he'd know it was me, anyway.

I take a deep breath, and my hand is shaking as I turn the door-knob. This Friday party idea has had me hopped up on adrenaline all morning. I'm sure it's just that and has nothing to do with how badly I want to see Mr. Knight. When I walk in, Mr. Knight glances up from his open laptop on his desk. His entire body pauses almost imperceptibly, which leads me to wonder if he's surprised to see me, but he recovers quickly so I don't know if that's good.

He clears his throat, and his voice is gruff. "Close the door behind you."

My mind short circuits for a moment and my pussy hums with her approval as I latch the door closed. Now that I'm in here, I have zero clue how to start the conversation. Neither of us speaks for about 30 seconds and we stare at each other. To hide my shaking hands, I clasp them behind my back and move my weight from one foot to the other. The longer the silence continues, the more tongue-tied I become. Why in the hell did he not ask me what I wanted when I walked in? Should I just blurt out, "tie me up, please, Sir?" I blush at the thought and open my mouth to say the words, but I can't.

Mr. Knight sighs and swivels his chair so his right arm leans against the desk. "Come kneel in front of me."

*Holy shit. Am I about to have a cock shoved in my throat?* I'm instantly wet as I kneel in front of him, and I try to slow down my excited breaths. None of the lawyers asked me for a blowjob yet and according to my husband, I'm fabulous at those. I'm eager to please Mr. Knight, so he'll continue wanting to tie me up. Determined to give him the best blowjob of his life, I kneel and wait.

When he doesn't immediately unzip his pants, disappointment stabs at my gut. I don't know how to tell him how amazing the Monday desk fuck was, and I thought that sucking on his cock might be a way to show my appreciation, or at least make myself more memorable. I don't want to examine my need for things to be different with Mr. Knight too closely, but the desire is there. With him, I want more than just a random office fuck.

But not only is he not moving, he's not speaking as I kneel and I gaze up at him, wide-eyed, expecting something—anything. Eventually he leans over and caresses my cheek. The cuff of his shirt rides up in that position, and I notice he has a yin and yang tattoo on his inner wrist. My heart pounds while I thrill at his touch, and my head spins a little when I try to contemplate the meaning of his tattoo. I want to question him, but it's like seeing a window into his soul and it feels too personal to ask since I hardly know him.

He rubs his thumb across my mouth, forcing my lower lip to pull down slightly, and I resist the urge to kiss his fingers.

"Do you know how beautiful you are?"

*Uh, what?* A sexual charge zings through my body and I flush. I don't answer him because I can't form a coherent thought. Being in this room alone and on my knees is oddly intimate. I should get up, give him the message, and leave. I'm not going to, though. I know myself too well. And the growing bulge in his trousers gives me hope I'll see some action.

Realizing that I shouldn't be here spurs me on and gives me courage, but I don't know how to ask him to let me suck him off. I can't exactly be all, "I notice you have a problem, let me take care of that for you." That might work for some girls, but I'm too awkward to make it sound sexy.

My brain finally figures out how to word it, and I softly stammer, "Is there anything you want from me?"

Since I'm still looking up at him, I see the wry smile before he replies. "Oh, Kitten, there is so much I want from you, but it's not my turn."

I'm thrilled at being called Kitten, so it takes a second for me to realize what he actually said. Wait, what? I was right about them having turns? That's crazy hot, but also not good for my immediate needs. My insistent pussy buzzes at me and wants more.

Before I lose my nerve, I whisper, "I won't tell anyone, I promise."

He lets out a soft snort and grins. When he leans back in his chair, it breaks the spell he has over me, and the energy in the room shifts from expectation to businesslike.

Mr. Knight's matter-of-fact tone confirms it. "I assume you are here to tell me you want to be tied up?"

I lick my lips before responding, "Yes, Sir."

He watches the tip of my tongue on my lips and just grins at me. "How would you prefer to be bound?"

Oh, uh, shit. I wasn't expecting to have options.

"Whatever you think is best is fine with me. I trust you."

Hearing that brings out the wry smile again, and he replies, "I'll think of something appropriate."

Knowing he's going to be thinking about different ways to tie me up delights me. Having him decide was the better move, and I didn't even plan it that way. Mr. Knight glances at his laptop, and I can tell I'm about to be dismissed.

"Okay, Kitten. I need to work and think of what I'm going to do to you tomorrow."

Since I'm now the subject of his thoughts, I'm not as disappointed to be leaving as I expected. I gracefully rise from my knees and leave. Neither of us says goodbye, but when I glance at him before closing the door, our eyes lock for a moment. He's the first one to break contact and it makes me smile, despite how rattled I am from the encounter.

I take the back hallways to avoid running into anyone. I want to sit there and gather my wits and keep the adrenaline going. At my desk, my instant messenger is flashing, and it's Mr. Jacobs telling me he plans to have dinner delivered for us on Friday and we'll have a picnic before the other fun. Oh shit, Jon doesn't get home until later than I do. He might miss the Zoom conference by the time he gets off work. I probably should have thought about my husband when planning this with my boss.

I shoot Jon a text to update him about the timing, and he quickly replies that he took the afternoon off and had already thought of the issue. I breathe a sigh of relief. Jon might be a goofy guy, but he's not dumb. Replying with a thumbs up sign, I set my phone aside and concentrate on work. I need to get more done today than normal because I'm positive not much work will get done tomorrow.

Right before lunchtime, Cindy approaches my desk and snips at me. "So I hear you guys are staying late tomorrow after work. I'm ordering dinner. What sandwich do you want from the deli?"

Uh, I think someone's panties are in a bunch for not being invited to the office party. There's a delicious deli down the street that most of us get lunch from regularly, so I rattle off my usual favorite. She writes it down and as she leaves; I swear I hear her mumble that she wouldn't mind some overtime as well.

I snicker as she disappears down the hall. Cindy, I don't think you're prepared for this type of overtime. Being amused by Cindy's attitude gives me the push to focus on work. I really want the party to go off without a hitch tomorrow, and that means I must be productive today.

By the time the day is over, Cindy seems to be out of her snit and she's cheerful as she says goodnight to me. I sit in my car for a few minutes before leaving, almost terrified of going home. I want this badly, but how am I going to sleep tonight? I also need to get home and take a long shower to shave everywhere. No way am I going with a prickly pussy since I shaved last weekend for Mr. Knight. I don't feel like getting frisky with Jon, so the shaving has to happen before he gets home. I'll spend tonight shaving and contemplating tomorrow. Maybe I need some new toenail polish? A few weeks ago I picked up a bright pink polish named Sinful Pink, and somehow it seems fitting.

# CHAPTER 2

Choosing my outfit on Friday morning was crazier than normal. I'm not sure why I didn't think about what to wear last night when I was just lounging around the house all in a dither about today. Jon was preoccupied as well, so he left me alone. He was off researching bondage on his computer and probably spanking the monkey and coming all over the rope I gave him from Mr. Knight.

I'm freshly shaven and my toes are pink, so I was semi-productive last night, but none of my clothes seem quite right. Forget "business casual", I need a "business slutty" dress. Is that a thing? Finally settling on my standard short black skirt and purple button-down blouse, I dig around in my shoe pile before selecting my sexiest black, strappy sandals. The skirt is so short, it almost feels indecent to go with bare legs, so I smooth on a pair of thigh-highs. I know at least one lawyer likes thigh-highs.

I've been mooning over Mr. Knight most of the week and I barely gave the other lawyers a thought, but they really all are sweet in their own way. No one has tried anything I didn't consent to first, and I've been getting my enjoyment from them, just as much as they are from me. Mr. Daniels, the new lawyer at the firm, was especially sweet and boyish... until he decided not to be. I shiver when I think back on him, taking control of the lightsaber inside my greedy snatch. I really should demonstrate to Jon how that looked one of these nights. It would thrill Jon to his geeky core to see me stuffed with his toy lightsaber.

Jon is singing show tunes in the shower when I leave. He's usually doing his own thing in the morning, so not kissing goodbye is pretty standard for us, but I could have used the reassurance of his arms around me this morning. Now that the day has arrived, I'm more nervous than I expected and the conference gang bang is still hours away.

I skip the latte since I'm jittery enough without a caffeine jolt. The work parking lot is oddly deserted when I get there, and when I enter the building and ask Cindy where everyone is, she just shrugs and ignores me. Guess I was wrong and someone is still in a snit after all. I honestly can't worry about Cindy's feelings today. I'm already half in a panic and I've only been in the office a few minutes. Deciding I'll bring her a gift card on Monday for a free lunch somewhere, I push her from my thoughts. I'll figure out something good this weekend that will thrill her.

When I switch on my computer, my hands are shaking. I need to calm the fuck down, since it's barely eight in the morning. A few months ago I attempted to learn meditation through an app on my phone, but after a few sessions I decided I wasn't a meditating type of girl. Plus, who wants Zen Miranda? Maybe my nervous energy is my charm? Or at least, that's what I told myself two months ago when I threw in the towel. My mind wanders too much to meditate, but I need the distraction currently, so I pop in my earbuds and tap open the app.

Soft beach sounds and seagulls lull me and I close my eyes, breathing deep. I didn't get a ton of sleep last night, and without the caffeine to keep me buzzed, as soon as I relax I drift off.

I'm snapped awake when a stack of files drops on my desk right in front of me. Cindy is glaring at me as I pull out the earbuds.

"Ugh, sorry, was trying to meditate." I try to sound contrite. I've never seen Cindy this annoyed before. She's usually the sweetest gal ever.

"Looked more like sleeping to me. Mr. Jacobs wants these finished before lunch." She huffs off and I'm left with a jumble of files that are way too many to do by lunchtime. What sort of game is he playing?

By the time lunch rolls around, I'm feeling grateful to Mr. Jacobs. I had zero chance to contemplate all my holes being stuffed later since I was too busy with work. The lawyers better talk amongst themselves because I don't want anyone thinking they are going to ass-fuck me tonight. I'm not ready for that yet. I haven't gotten the extra fingers inside me that Mr. Parks promised, so an actual dick shoved in isn't appealing. Even when playing with Jon at home, he's hesitant to do much else than one thick finger.

Just thinking about fingers in my ass makes me wet and I squirm in my chair a little. I'm going to be a quivering mess by the time work is over. I'm too worked up to eat lunch, so I nibble on almonds at my desk. At around 1 p.m. Cindy grumbles up to me and informs me she's sick and going home, and that she's transferred the switchboard to me. My mouth drops open, but she doesn't stick around long enough for me to reply and as soon as she walks down the hall, the phone rings.

Well, fuck her and the horse she rode in on. As I take phone call after phone call—because I guess everyone calls their lawyer on a Friday afternoon—I don't have time to dwell much on the Cindy problem. Maybe I'll get the guts up to tell the guys at dinner that they need to buy her an employee appreciation gift card. Her level of hurt seems beyond what a simple free lunch will fix. Plus her actual issue isn't with me, it's with the lawyers who didn't ask her to stay, so they should be the ones to pony up the gift.

When the phones finally die down and it's time to close up shop, I'm slightly light-headed from lack of food and high emotions. I pack up my desk, but I'm uncertain what they want me to do. Am I supposed to just go to the conference room?

I'm digging through my purse, looking for anything to nibble on, when Mr. Knight approaches my desk with a sandwich bag. Ooooh, my hero! He lays the bag on my desk and examines me with a critical eye. I flush, but immediately open the bag, hoping he'll leave so I can wolf the sandwich down. I try to hide my shaking hands, but it's hard to get it unwrapped.

"Stop," Mr. Knight demands harshly. He takes the sandwich from me, unwraps it, and hands it back to me while he pulls the chair from the opposite side of the desk around next to mine. He sits and watches me take a couple of bites, slowly chew, and swallow.

"Kitten, did you eat lunch?" His voice is softer, and I like this version of Mr. Knight better.

I shrug. "I only nibbled on almonds."

He sighs before replying. "Eat up. I want to prep you in my office, but you need some time to digest and get your blood sugar normal first."

While I eat, he explains his plan for tonight. He's going to hobble my elbows behind my back, but leave my legs free. He said he doesn't want to push me because this might be overwhelming. As he's explaining exactly how he plans to restrain my elbows, I notice the cuffs of his shirt are unbuttoned and he's rolled up his sleeves. It exposes his yin and yang tattoo again, and before I can stop myself; I reach over and caress the outline. He traps my fingers against his arm and lifts them up to his lips to give them a kiss before releasing them.

A shiver runs down my spine and I forget to chew. I try to breathe normally from the feathery kiss, but I'm slightly trembling.

Mr. Knight's cool eyes regard me for a minute, and I flush under his gaze. When he speaks, his voice is quiet, and I can tell he doesn't want anyone to overhear. "Kitten, we can't do this. You know that, right?"

Every time he calls me Kitten I get a zing of pleasure, but this time there is a flash of pain as well. I was hoping my feelings could be the elephant in the room that no one acknowledged. But guess he needs to make sure I know I'm just an office fuck.

I pout a little, trying to pretend I'm not hurt. "Yes, I know."

"Miranda, look at me." His voice is still quiet, but commanding.

I glance up at him and hold his gaze. "Yes?"

"You're married, we work at the same employer, and four men are fucking you. We can't do this."

Wait, which part is his biggest problem? I don't have the nerve to ask him, so I finish my sandwich quietly. When I'm finished, he and I walk silently to his office. He closes the door and almost looks apologetically at me.

"You're going to have to take off your blouse and bra."

*Oooh, uh, okay?* I thrill a little at this thought because the conference room is on the other end of the building. I know it's only me and the four lawyers here, but imagining myself walking down the hallways with my breasts exposed is slutty and awesome.

I make quick work of removing my purple blouse and bra and I stand in the middle of the room, waiting. He's holding a long folded double length of rope, and I shiver as he moves behind me. He takes a moment to tell me exactly what he plans to do, and yet when he makes the first loop around my elbows, I'm shocked at how erotically vulnerable the knowledge is that you're standing there letting someone restrain you.

Mr. Knight is methodical in his movements, and while he's taking his time, I can tell he's done this many times before and he's probably going a lot faster than most people would. I can't see what's happening. The rope bites my skin, and it doesn't take long before he's finishing up and tying off the ends to what he called a simple elbow tie. It doesn't feel simple to me when I give an experimental soft shoulder tug and my elbows are pretty firmly connected with whatever snazzy rope magic he's done. It's not wholly uncomfortable. He didn't pull my arms too tight behind me. I'd say it's the right amount of discomfort currently, but it could progress to being worse as time goes on.

Mr. Knight surprises me and kisses my shoulder before leading me out of the office. He doesn't offer me any cover-up and I try to stand up straight as I walk, flaunting my still pert breasts. If I'm going to be the office slut, I might as well own it. I've been wet all day and the half-naked stroll is making me more turned on with each step. Are they all waiting for me in the conference room? Will they have clothes on?

The conference room door is closed and we pause in front of it. Mr. Knight looks down at me and I glance up at him.

"Are you ready for this?" I don't answer and just nod.

# CHAPTER 3

Mr. Jacobs, Mr. Parks, and Mr. Daniels are all sitting in chairs, relaxed and laughing at a joke one of them told before we walked in. As we come in, they all get quiet and stare at me. I have the uncomfortable realization that I'm a minnow in a sea of sharks. At least my legs aren't bound, so I can run if I decide to.

I have an insane urge to giggle at the thought of me busting out the front doors of the office, boobs first, with my elbows tied behind me. How would I flag down a car for help?

Mr. Knight leads me to the conference table and boosts me up so I'm sitting on the edge. He leans over and runs his hands down my stockings and gently pulls one shoe off. Uh, wait... we aren't going to talk? We're just going straight for this? As soon as he removes my other shoe, he reaches for the side zipper on my skirt as a wave of panic threatens to wash over me.

I want to tell him to stop, thatI'm not ready, but I can't find my voice. My shortness of breath, chilly hands, and the fluttering in my stomach tip me off that a panic attack might be imminent. It only ramps up as Mr. Knight tugs my skirt off from underneath my ass and I'm left sitting in my blue satin panties and black thigh highs.

Whose smart idea was this, anyway? I can't remember the reasons I said yes.

Mr. Knight must finally sense something because he puts his hand on my cheek and tips my face up to look into my eyes.

"Miranda, you doing okay?" His voice is gentle, but does little to soothe me.

I don't want to admit how close to panic I am, but when I try to nod my head yes, it's a weird head bobble instead.

Just at that moment, I hear Jon's voice behind me. I try to turn but it's awkward so I can't tell what it's coming from. Mr. Parks walks around the table with a laptop, and the sense of relief at seeing Jon's face on the screen almost makes me cry.

"Hey, Miranda. Are you doing okay?" Jon is cheerful and smiling through the camera. I nod at him as he continues. "Baby, I'm so hard right now. You look amazing. They have you set up on the overhead cameras and I can see the room from different angles as I click around."

As he says that, I look up and around the room, and, sure enough, there are multiple cameras on the ceiling. I haven't been to any tele-conference meetings and we have a tech service that comes in to take care of all our needs, so I know little about the setup.

"I want you to know that I'm going to be thinking about you and how hot you look, and stroking myself." The longer he talks to me, the more at ease I feel. "And when you get home, we'll snuggle for as long as you want." By the time he mentions snuggling, a small grin tugs at the corner of my mouth.

Mr. Parks tells Jon he's moving the laptop to the side table and Jon blows me air kisses. Letting me see Jon was the perfect way to calm me down. I've been looking forward to this since they offered it, and if I chickened out and left, I'd always regret it.

When Mr. Jacobs takes the lead and moves close to me to stand between my legs, I'm feeling prepared for whatever happens. Except maybe not more than two fingers in my ass, please.

# CHAPTER 4

Mr. Jacobs pushes my shoulders down gently until I'm laying on my back on the conference table. The surface is cold and I glance up at the cream-colored ceiling and wonder which camera Jon is watching from right now. Knowing my husband, it's the one with the best view so I give a big smile towards that camera, hoping I'm right.

Fingers hook along my panties' edge, and I look down to see Mr. Jacobs stripping them off me and tossing them aside. I'm naked other than my stockings now, and the immediate moisture between my legs tells me that my pussy isn't unhappy. Clothes are rustling and I glance around trying to see what is happening, but I only catch brief glimpses of bodies at the end of the table past my head. It sounds like they are all removing their clothes, and Mr. Jacobs, still stationed in front of me, is stripping.

Wow. This really IS happening. I squirm a little when the now-naked Mr. Jacobs hooks me by my knees and pulls me more towards the edge of the table.

"Miranda, I'm going to fuck you first, but I will not come. We're going to take turns with you and none of us will come until the end. We're going to shower you with our cum."

My brain freezes for a good five seconds. HOLY SHIT. This is possibly the dirtiest thing anyone has ever said to me. The buzzing neediness between my legs tells me that my pussy is 100 percent on board with the party plans. If she had her own marching band parade, they would be headed down main street and ready for the key event. My pussy lips are throbbing to some imaginary beat and I'm hoping he just grabs me and rams straight into me. I need to be fucked NOW.

When he spreads my legs, cool air hits my slick gash, but it's quickly replaced by Mr. Jacobs probing his thick tip against my hole. I don't even have time to thank Jesus before he's pushing inside me, slow and deep.

"Aaah aah," I moan as he fully sheaths himself and pauses. His cock is probably my favorite out of all the lawyers, but I would never admit it to anyone—not even Jon. Once I adjust, he grabs my hips and starts pumping away. My hands behind my back do not make this position comfortable, and I know I will not come with Mr. Jacobs. I have no way to brace myself, and I'm getting knocked around with every plunge.

The room is quiet, other than my moaning and Mr. Jacob's slight puffing and grunting as he fucks me. I have a brief thought about Jon and what he's feeling right now, but knowing my twisted husband like I do, I bet he's wanking it and thrilled.

Mr. Jacobs pulls out suddenly.

"I'm done."

His matter-of-fact answer about being done with me jolts me again with a twisted pleasure. I didn't realize how much I delight at being a dirty slut. I knew I liked to call myself a slut, but this circle jerk conference room fuck fest is on a whole new level of sluttiness.

Mr. Daniels replaces Mr. Jacobs, and I wonder if the order was pre-arranged. I get a good look at his beautiful golden brown skin before he stands between my legs and rams his cock straight into me, setting a fast and furious pace. Oh shit, this is not the same gentle man who I had to seduce the other day. This is a side of him I hadn't seen before, and it's fucking amazing. I try to glimpse everyone in the room, but all I can see is Mr. Jacobs standing behind and to the side of Mr. Daniels, his massive cock in his hand while he strokes himself slowly, watching every thrust from Mr. Daniels.

I don't know how easily I forgot Mr. Daniels and his beautiful cock. I take back what I said about Mr. Jacobs, THIS right here is hands down my favorite lawyer cock. The veins on the shaft are so thick, they feel like ribs and I chant, "Oh, my God," while he fucks me. I'm getting close to coming when he pulls out, and I cry out in disappointment. What the fuck man, they need to let me come.

The brief thought flashes in my head to wonder who's going to be next, but when Mr. Knight appears, fully naked, a zing of pleasure shoots from my pussy to my brain. Mr. Knight stands over me, smiles gently, but when he motions to someone to come help him, I'm confused. When Mr. Daniels comes back into my vision, it becomes clear what the plan is. They both help flip me over and then Mr. Daniels backs away.

Mr. Knight pulls my legs far enough off the table where I can stand on my tiptoes. I must look a sight with my arms bound behind me, thigh-highs on, bent over the surface of the conference table. When Mr. Knight steps up and uses the tip of his cock to draw circles on my ass cheek, I'm ready for him to fuck me.

I expect him to plunge straight in, but he pushes my legs open further and brings his hand between my legs to rub my clit in soft circles. Jesus Christ! Not expecting the gentleness, I cry out in pleasure and press back against his hand. He stops rubbing my clit and instead brings his cock up to tease me. He presses in briefly and pulls out, repeatedly. Each time he removes the tip, I make a tiny whimper. I can't take much more of this. I'm ready to come, and he needs to fuck me. When he does it again, I can't help myself.

"Please, Sir, fuck me!"

He growls loud and clear, "As you wish, Kitten," while he plunges straight to my core. The shock of him using "Kitten" in front of the cameras where my husband just heard is replaced with intense sexual pleasure. I moan long and loud as he grinds his member into me, pressing against my ass with each thrust.

My breasts are flat against the table, but Mr. Knight yanks on the binding between my arms and pulls my chest off the table slightly so that my hard nipples are grazing the surface with each plunge. I'm moaning and wishing I could press back against him better, but I have no leverage, so I have to just take whatever he wants to give me.

I'm going to come soon, but before I can, he pulls out. He keeps hold of the rope with one hand, and curves his other around my stomach. I'm confused at what is happening until another set of hands grabs me and I'm being moved off the table. They shove me to my knees, and Mr. Knight kneels behind me, still holding the rope, and fucks me again.

I close my eyes and moan loudly, but pop them back open when a cock brushes my cheek. My favorite ass-finger lawyer, Mr. Parks, is guiding his cock to my mouth while Mr. Knight still fucks me from behind. I'd considered this could be a possible scenario, but the reality is WAY better than what I imagined.

I willingly open my mouth as he guides his boner past my lips and down my throat. I've seen porn videos of this before, but I didn't fully appreciate how someone pounding against your ass thrusts you forward onto another man's rod deep in your throat. Mr. Parks face fucks me harder than I expect, while Mr. Knight thrusts faster behind me. For a moment the rough cock in my throat reminds me of being on my knees in my neighbor, Harold's, bedroom while Harold face fucked me hard and used me as his birthday gift. I have the same glorious sluttiness now as I did then, while the two lawyers tag team my various holes.

Mr. Park's cock in my mouth muffles my loud moans and spurs me to greater heights as Mr. Knight pounds away behind me. I can't chant my usual "Oh, my God," right as I come, but the orgasm hits me hard as the face fucking muffles my garbled screams.

Waves of pleasure wash over me and my entire body shakes and quivers as I ride the peak and stars explode behind my eyes. I'm still moaning and trembling when both men pull out of my various holes and lay me down on my back on the conference room floor. I open my eyes and my vision is slightly darkened when all four men move over me and block some of the overhead lights.

They are all standing there, jerking off while I'm a quivering mess on the floor. They fill the room with sounds of moaning, panting, and slight groans. I keep my eyes open and Mr. Jacobs is the first to come. His jizz spurts across my chest and a warm drizzle hits my nipple. Seeing him coat me with his cum must have been the tipping point for everyone else, because after that it becomes a milky white waterfall all around me as they collectively groan and spurt their seed. Some lands in my hair, on my stomach, my legs. Some trickles down my cheek. Since they tied my hands behind me, there is nothing I can do but lie still as it drips off me.

They all grunt and jerk until their tanks are empty. One by one they all slump into conference chairs, drained, and I continue to lie on the floor, content. I focus my vision on the closest ceiling camera and smile up at it. I hope Jon is getting an excellent shot of all this cum covering me because I know without a doubt that his love for me is the only reason I could experience this.

# CHAPTER 5

## Epilogue

When I get home from the party, Jon is waiting for me at the door. Crusty cum coats my face and arms, but he engulfs me in a bear hug as soon as I walk in.

"God, Kitten, I love you so much. That was amazing."

When he uses my pet name, a restlessness within me soothes. He's not upset about Mr. Knight calling me Kitten.

Jon steps back, giving me a critical eye while holding my hands. "How was it for you, babe?"

I pause, uncertain how to explain the mixed emotions running through me. It was incredibly hot, but scary, and not as intimate as I prefer for sex. I found more meaning in my one-on-one sessions with my bosses, so I'm not sure I would seek another big event soon. But as an occasional treat? I could see myself doing it again.

Giving Jon's hand a squeeze, I simply say, "I had fun, but it was a lot to take in. I might wait a bit before doing it again."

Jon laughs. "I don't blame you. It seemed intense from my view as well. But are you glad you did it?"

Am I glad? I think for a moment. Yes, it was an experience I'll never forget.

"Jon, you goof. Of course, I'm glad. Did you see how awesome that looked?"

He kisses my forehead, which makes me smile and wonder if he just kissed some dried cum. Jon has the bathroom ready for me to take a shower, with a fluffy blue towel laid out and my robe hanging on the door. He leaves me alone to shower, and as I soap myself up fully, scrubbing the cum off, I think about how my life has changed.

There aren't many husbands who would allow their wife to fuck other men and be so into it, and Jon is an amazing and sweet guy. No matter what allure Mr. Knight holds over me, Jon is my anchor and tonight proves it. At the end of it all, it was Jon I was thinking about as I was lying on the floor, and Jon was the one I wanted to rush home to.

I'm tired as I get out of the shower, and the idea of snuggling in bed with my thoughtful and wonderful husband is the best idea in the world to me. No matter where I go in the future with my hotwife plans, I want Jon to be there when I get home.

The End

# HAROLD'S HOTWIFE BIRTHDAY

# CHAPTER 1

I glance out the kitchen window at my neighbor, Harold, mowing his lawn as he religiously does every Sunday. I enjoy sleeping in on weekends and he likes to mow at 9 a.m. sharp every Sunday. So when he wakes me up, I grumble about how the Church of Harold is in service while my husband, Jonathan, only laughs at me and brings me coffee.

In reality I don't mind, because I enjoy peeking out the window and watching Harold mow. He's in his late forties and has this older man, hot dad vibe going on that my pussy really seems to dig. I've also heard him speak before and he's got a cute southern accent, which adds to the appeal. I'd totally shag Harold any day of the week.

Ever since my husband opened up about his hotwife fantasies and I fucked my lawyer bosses at work, my honey pot has been working overtime whenever she spies something that turns her on. Lately it's been older men with gray hair. Harold and his wife, Vickie, have lived in the neighborhood for years longer than we have and they have a couple of grown kids and way too many pets. We don't socialize with them much, other than a friendly wave and a Christmas card.

I've noticed Jon checking out Vickie occasionally. She's in her forties, voluptuous, and radiates sensuality. It doesn't hurt she's a natural redhead to boot since that ups her hotness factor by 10 for Jon. He once tried to get me to dye my brown hair a bright red, but since I wasn't willing to maintain it, there was no point. I told him to just watch a bunch of porn with redheads to satisfy that itch. From what I can tell by our computer browser history, he's complied nicely with that command.

I sip my coffee while peeking out from behind the curtains and silently curse that Harold is keeping his shirt on today. I think this hotwife deal I've got going on with Jon is messing with my head. Intellectually I know Harold isn't some tremendous prize in the looks department, but something about that slightly soft belly and nerdy glasses along with his gray hair really buzzes me. I've noticed him watching me occasionally when I'm outside, not in a pervy way, but I could still sense the approval in his glance. Being an attractive twenty-eight-year-old, gravity has not taken effect, so everything is still nice and firm. I enjoy being ogled a bit, and I purposely dress in tight clothing to attract attention. Jon gets his jollies when he thinks other guys are checking me out, so bonus points for dressing a little slutty every once in a while..

"Miranda, are you spying on Harold again?"

I jump a little when my husband walks in and accuses me of doing the exact thing I was doing.

I give him an impish grin and brandish my cup of coffee towards Jon. "Of course not. SEE, I'm drinking coffee and enjoying my morning."

"Uh, huh. Right."

Jon just grins at me as he passes through the kitchen and heads towards the garage. Every Sunday he spends the morning tinkering around doing whatever men do for hours in a garage. Pretty sure he just strokes the tools in his toolbox and pretends he knows how to use them. Nothing ever gets fixed or accomplished, but my husband is too adorable for me to care. Hell, for all I know he might have an old nudie magazine collection stashed out there and Sunday is his personal alone time.

I'm slightly wet, and I'm not sure if it's from watching Harold mow or if it's the thought of my husband wanking it alone every Sunday morning that's arousing. Jon has plenty of sexual energy for me since I started fucking my bosses, so I don't mind if he still takes personal time. I'm getting more than my fair share of sex.

I am slightly guilty about all the fun I've been having while he gets none, but Jon acts more than content. He's sexually charged and thrilled at a level he's never been in our marriage. Who knew that all I had to do was boink a bunch of men to make my husband happy. Life is too good currently, and I keep waiting for the other shoe to drop. I hate to be the type who expects the worst, but I'm honestly too delighted with my life right now and it feels wrong.

I sigh and move away from the window. I have a list of things to get done today because I slacked yesterday while my husband did all his weekend chores. Now he gets to have a fun Sunday while I will be the one slaving away. I quickly review my mental list of what I need to do and when I think about the flowerbeds that need weeding, a tingle zips down my spine. I think now would be the perfect time to do some gardening.

# CHAPTER 2

In five minutes flat, I'm outside bent over a flower bed in a pink tank top and the shortest pair of black shorts I own. The weeds really do need to be removed, so I'm wearing gardening gloves and have a bright orange bucket and tiny trowel with me to hack at any tough roots. I hate to admit that it's been a week too long on getting out here, but I've been a busy girl lately and needed to recuperate on my weekends. Making sure my ass stays angled towards Harold and Vickie's house, I keep myself busy pulling out any invading vegetation.

When I stand up and arch my back to stretch and move to another area, I notice Harold facing me, making yet another pass across his yard with the mower. He doesn't smile and his intense stare gives me a pleasant buzz. Despite his stern expression, I grin and wave my fingers at him in a cutesy manner. I'm able to coax a slight grin from him, which delights me. I wanted to tease him a little, not make him cranky. Pretending to ignore him, I bend over another flowerbed and continue my task. I can feel his eyes on me, and my pleasure pit is wet and ready for action.

Jon and I rarely have sex on Sunday mornings, and I realize I came out here to tease Harold, but I'm probably torturing myself more.

Whose bright idea was this? The hum from my core tells me that maybe my pussy is driving my bus more often than I like to admit. I accuse my husband of always thinking with his cock, but maybe I'm guilty of the same thing since I'm outside on a warm Sunday morning in tiny shorts and swinging my ass at my neighbor.

As I take the filled bucket to the yard waste bin on the side of the house, I notice the garage door is open and Vickie is standing in the entrance chatting with Jon. I dump the weeds and turn to head back to pull more when Jonathan spots me.

Jon's voice booms out, "Hey, Miranda. Come here a second."

I wipe the sweat off my forehead with my arm and saunter over to the pair. Vickie is stepping from foot to foot and worrying a piece of paper between her fingers. I briefly wonder what's got her so rattled, but quickly dismiss the thought because it's not my business.

When I get close, Jon drops his voice to a mock whisper. "Vickie wants to know if you would help with her husband's birthday."

Um, what? My brain takes two seconds to try and figure out what I could do for Harold for his birthday. I mean, I hardly know the guy.

I'm a little hesitant when I reply. "Uh, sure. What can I help with?"

I immediately assume she needs help decorating a cake or throwing a surprise party and needs me to be over there to let the guests in. When Vickie glances uncertainly at Jon and doesn't answer me, I suspect something bigger is afoot.

"Miranda, don't be angry..."

Jon knows I dislike it when he starts conversations like that because I immediately become angry. It's never followed up with anything good so far. I tell myself to chill and hear him out. It wouldn't do to get cranky in front of Vickie. I can wait until later to chew him out. Instead, I just glare at Jon. This better be good.

"So Vickie and I were talking last week, and I told her about our agreement."

My brain freezes. *Wait, what agreement is he talking about?* He's not talking about THE agreement with my bosses, is he? My eyes go round as saucers, and I'm guessing my face is displaying a slideshow of ten different emotions.

My expression quickly makes Jon realize he made a tactical error. "It's not bad, Miranda. Vickie and Harold used to do something similar in their younger years."

Somehow in my dear husband's messed-up logic, just because the neighbors used to be kinky means it's okay to spread our shit across the neighborhood? I'm a weird mixture of embarrassed, mad, and slightly turned on. Harold could bang other women at one time in their marriage? My esteem for Harold rises a few notches. I thought we were living next door to June and Ward Cleaver, but in reality we're living next to our future selves. At some point, it's going to be me in my late forties talking about the crazy shit I did in my twenties. Since the idea of Harold boinking other women is pleasing, I am more than willing to hear what my husband has to say next.

"It's Harold's birthday today and Vickie is wondering if you would be his present."

Uh... my brain has two simultaneous thoughts: *holy fuck, that's hot,* and *what the frick?* I side-eye my husband to gauge his reaction, and the absolute glee on his face tells me all I need to know. He wants me to do it. My pussy clenches and a zing of excitement thrills me to my toes.

I don't give myself time to second guess myself. I blurt out, "Yes!"

# CHAPTER 3

Jon and Vickie work out the details after I agree, but my brain is too mushy to pay attention. I leave them outside to strategize while I wander inside the house in a daze. There are so many reasons this is a horrible idea, but I push them back to the furthest corner of my mind. Right now I want to fuck Harold like I've never wanted to fuck anyone in my life. I hadn't even considered him as a viable option. He was just an older man who, for some odd reason, thrilled me whenever I saw him or we had brief contact. Did I really just agree to sleep with him? TONIGHT?

I'm in slight shock, sitting on the couch, when Jon comes in looking pleased with himself. He spots me and perches on the arm to explain the plan. Vickie is going to make Harold shower and get dressed, thinking he's going to a birthday dinner. But when he's ready, she's going to tell him I'm coming over to fuck him instead. Vickie will spend a couple of hours at our house watching a movie with Jon to give us some privacy.

This entire plan seems super weird, but based on the wetness in my panties, I don't care. I hope Harold is going to be okay with this birthday gift. How embarrassing will it be if he declines and Vickie has to come over here to call it off? How will I ever show my face to the neighbors again? I'm breathless and tingling. Please, just don't say no.

The rest of the afternoon is a bit of a blur. Jon is practically skipping around the house and telling me he wants all the details later tonight. He hints I better be up for round two when I get home. Before I know it, I'm showered and dressed in my sluttiest tiny black dress, with no bra or underwear. Jon picked out my wardrobe for tonight. He instructed me to wear the black dress, my sterling silver necklace that spells out the word 'Kitten' and my tallest pair of heels. I slip on some four-inch spiked high heels while Jon whistles at me from the bedroom doorway.

"You are one fine woman, Miranda. You might give him a heart attack as soon as he sees you."

His praise and obvious approval warms me. I love how supportive he is of me exploring my sexuality. I know that when I get home tonight, I'll willingly open my legs for him—or whatever else he chooses. The bonding time I get with Jon after an extramarital romp is just as important to me as it is to him. I need the connection to ground me and remind me that no matter what I'm doing with anyone else, Jon is my heart and home.

But that doesn't mean that right now I'm not horny as all hell and eager to fuck Harold. The doorbell chimes and Jon claps his hands like a little girl and practically squeals. I just smile at the back of my goofy husband as he sprints off to let Vickie in. I descend the stairs precariously and question why I didn't wait to put on my heels. Thank god I'm only walking next door. I haven't worn these shoes in a long time, and I may retire them after tonight. I think I'm getting too old for four-inch heels.

Vickie is standing just inside the door and gazing up at me with sparkling eyes as I join her.

"Wow, Miranda. You look amazing. Harold is going to flip."

Her response answered my unasked question. I guess Harold is down to fuck me. I look around for Jon but he calls to Vickie from the kitchen, asking if she wants anything to drink for the movie. She laughs and yells back that water is fine, and then turns to me and tells me Harold is waiting.

As I'm reaching to open the door to wobble my way to her house, she grabs my hand and squeezes it gently. She whispers "He likes to be called Sir."

My breath catches as she drops my hand and hurries off to join Jon in the kitchen. I glance at her retreating backside and I'm struck again by how sensual she is. She must really love her husband. I'm still not sure I could share Jon, though I have been warming up to the idea lately. If he really wanted to, I might consider trying it once to see how it goes. But I think I'll wait until he brings it up. So far he's been perfectly happy with me screwing around and coming home to him. If that's really all he wants, I won't rock the boat.

I walk slowly next door, partly because I can't walk any faster in these shoes, but also because I need time to prepare myself. Where is he going to fuck me? Is he going to do me in the bed he shares with his wife? This is my first time having sex outside of my office with someone other than my husband, and I'm a little intimidated. Not knowing what I'm doing or how I'm going to have sex seems to be a kink of mine, and every time a new sexual encounter comes up with a new person, I get extra excited and wet. Today is no different. By the time I reach their front door and ring the bell, I'm shivering in anticipation.

When the door opens, Harold is standing on the other side. He's wearing grey slacks and a light blue button-down shirt, but no shoes. His white socks peek out from under his pant legs. The contrast between his wholesome appearance and my tight little black number creates a divide, and I gloriously feel like a slut. I'm literally some guy's birthday gift. How awesome is this?

Harold clears his throat, but doesn't smile. "Hello, Miranda."

My wet pussy clenches when I hear my name with his southern accent, while an unexpected wave of shyness washes over me. I softly croon, "Happy birthday, Sir."

# CHAPTER 4

Harold moves back and to the side, holding the door open for me while I attempt to strut into the foyer. Their house has a similar floor plan to ours, so I know the bedroom is upstairs. Damn Jon and his desire for me to look slutty for the neighbor—I might kill myself if I attempt more stairs in these shoes.

Harold's thoughts mimic mine because he snickers. "Why don't you take those shoes off? While you ARE sexy in them, I don't want you to kill yourself on my account."

I gratefully kick them off, though removing them produces an oddly vulnerable emotion. I only have one item of clothing on, now that I've removed my shoes, since my Kitten necklace doesn't count. The only thing standing between Harold seeing my entire naked body is this black dress.

Harold assesses me with a steady gaze, and despite having my dress on, I feel exposed.

"Are you sure you want to do this?" His voice is husky and the bulge in his pants grows the longer he stares at me.

Seeing him grow hard heightens my excitement.

"Yes, Sir." I'm not sure how often he enjoys being called "Sir", but I'm getting a nice charge every time I say it, so I may continue to use it all night long unless told otherwise.

Harold approaches, and I shiver when he gets close enough for me to feel the warmth of his body. He reaches out and traces the Kitten necklace. His rough finger along the edge of the necklace brushes my skin, electric, while my stomach flutters and I sway towards him.

He grins playfully. "Okay, Kitten. Let's go upstairs."

I'm jolted when he uses my husband's pet name for me. Jon doesn't realize what happens when I wear this necklace during sexual encounters. It happened once before with my boss and I didn't tell. I won't tell him this time either. Hearing Harold say it in that sexy southern accent of his, and my instinctive response of wanting to do whatever he tells me to do after saying it, gives birth to the idea that I might wear this necklace more often now. This is twice now it's been surprisingly erotic, and if other men want to call me Kitten because of a necklace... who am I to deny them that pleasure?

Harold pursues me up the stairs and knowing he's inspecting my ass produces a smirk. I want to blurt out, *"Yes, this is the same ass I was bending over for you earlier,"* but stay quiet. The idea of fucking him is exhilarating, and I hope he's as aroused as I am. Based on the small amount of chitchat and how fast he ushered me upstairs, I'm guessing he is.

We pass the master bedroom and until the moment we do, I didn't realize how the thought of fucking him in their marital bed was bugging me. He directs me to a spare room with a queen-sized bed as I breathe a slight sigh of relief and relax. As the tension drains away, I turn to him with a smile.

I attempt to give him my best doe-eyed innocent look, though I think my outfit might ruin any chaste vibe. "Since it's your birthday, Sir. What would you like?"

His voice is stern when he replies. "I want you to take your clothes off and get on your knees."

*Oh hell, yes!* My inner goddess does a happy dance. It almost seems impossible, but I become more wet. If he keeps this up, I'm going to have lubrication running down my thigh. I quickly strip off my dress and toss it across the room. All concern about my lack of underclothes flies from my head as I stand in front of him, gloriously naked. His intake of breath tells me he probably expected a bra and panties. I drop to my knees eagerly and wait.

Harold slowly unbuttons his shirt and removes it, exposing the love handles I've been drooling over for months. I really don't know why it's such a draw, but I want to wrap my arms around his stomach and kiss his chest. I know I'm not odd in this desire. Plenty of friends talk about how older men with softer bodies are an enormous turn on to them. It probably has something to do with the combination of sexual experience and the acceptance a woman gets from an older man. They don't expect us to be perfect.

I'm restless and Harold is taking too long to get undressed. Since I'm on my knees, I assume he wants my mouth on his cock and I'm greedy to taste him. I crawl towards him and grasp for his belt.

He laughs and steps back out of reach. "What an impatient little Kitten you are."

I sit back on my heels and pout at him. Fine, we'll play it his way! Based on the size of the bulge in his pants, I'm sure he's having a tough time being slow. But it's possible he also likes to torture himself. He removes his belt and unzips his slacks, letting them fall to the floor. He's left standing there in blue plaid boxers and white socks. The boxers don't have a button on them, so the head of his cock is peeking out. I lick my lips in anticipation. What is taking this guy so long? Doesn't he want to feel my mouth around him?

He strips off the boxers, but leaves his socks on when he approaches me. I find it oddly endearing that he doesn't take them off. His cock is fully erect and curved upwards. He's not huge, but he's big enough that I know he's going to hit all the right spots if given the chance. I had a fantasy of being on my back with my arms crossed above my head, while he's pinning my wrists down, so I'm torn about the implied blow job request when he told me to get on my knees. But it's his birthday, and the birthday boy always gets what he wants. I don't have time to dwell on it because he puts his hands on my head and guides my lips to his cock.

I grab the base of his shaft while licking the tip of his member. I love being on my knees when giving blowjobs because it gives me access to play with all the delightful bits. Keeping a firm grip on his knob with one hand, I run my fingers gently around his fun bag while I continue to just kiss and lick the tip. He bunches his hands in my hair, which signals to me that his patience has worn thin. I look up at him and he's staring down at me as I open my mouth fully to engulf his cock.

As soon as he's past my teeth, he takes control and pumps against me, forcing me to face fuck him. My husband is never this rough, but something in me thrills at being used for Harold's pleasure. I'm still using one hand to keep hold of his shaft while he thrusts and forces his rod deep into my throat. I have a moment of being thankful he's not larger because if he was, I'd be choking on his cock. Since he's not, it's exciting, and the pressure on my head isn't so hard that I wouldn't be able to back away if I really wanted to. But I don't—I'm getting more aroused, and as I reach my free hand down between my legs to massage my wet clit in circles I moan around his cock.

I glance up at him again and his eyes are closed, with a pained expression on his face that edges on pleasure. I rub my hand down his shaft to his sack again and give it a gentle tug. Knowing it's iffy on whether guys like that, I don't yank hard, but he doesn't complain and presses against my mouth harder, so I know whatever I'm doing is fine. His shaft jerks a little and I can tell he's about to come when he releases my hair and withdraws fully from my mouth.

"Jesus." He swears a little, as if he almost lost control or can't believe what's happening to him.

He's slightly breathless, and points to the bed. "Up on the edge, on your knees."

"Yes, Sir!" I quickly climb up and position myself on the edge, looking over my shoulder at him and wiggling my ass. This isn't my fantasy of being pinned down, but being fucked from behind is just as good.

Brushing his member against my ass, he caresses my slick folds with his fingers and slips two digits inside me. I gasp and undulate against his hand, silently thanking the gods that he wants to bone me. I have zero problems giving blow jobs, but if this is my one chance with Harold, I want his cock buried deep inside me.

He removes his fingers and replaces them with the tip of his shaft. For a man who just almost came in my mouth, he sure has more patience suddenly. I expected him to ram straight into me, but he's teasing my hole, moving in and out slowly. I moan and press back against him the next time he attempts to slide it in only partially, and force him in deeper. Feeling my cave walls stretch around him unleashes the beast in him, and he plunges in fully until he bottoms out.

"Oh, my god!" I half squeal as he sets a steady pace and grabs my hips for leverage. It didn't seem like I got much warm-up, but this entire time with him has been such a turn-on, I was more than ready for him. I lower my arms down so I'm on my elbows, instead of my hands, to force a change to the angle of his thrusts. It also widens the area so I can feel his ball sack hitting against my clit with every plunge.

Jesus Christ, this is amazing. I'm not sure if it's because I've always secretly wanted to fuck him, or if he's just amazing in bed, but I'm edging closer and closer to my orgasm. The spasm starts deep in my core.

"Oooh, I'm going to come!" I pant out at him and moan loudly.

"Be a good Kitten and come for me," he demands.

Harold's sexy southern voice tips me over the abyss and I shudder, rocking against him as waves of pleasure ripple through me. He picks up the pace, and with several sharp thrusts and a soft moan, he explodes, coating my inner walls with his hot cum. He jerks against me several times, unloading every drop of jizz into my greedy, grasping box.

When he has no more to give me, Harold pulls out and lies down on his back next to me on the bed while I slump to my side, facing him, too relaxed and limp to do much else. He turns to look at me, a soft smile on his lips and a sparkle in his eye. He reaches out and tucks my mussed hair behind my ear.

I nuzzle into his palm, "Was I a wonderful birthday present, Sir?"

He grins. "You were the best birthday gift I've ever received."

We both lay there, slightly dozing, until the downstairs door opens and Vickie calls out. "Is it safe to come home?"

Harold laughs and yells out, "We're done. It's safe."

I'm more than a little uncomfortable with Vickie coming in here while I'm naked, so I quickly snatch up my dress and shimmy into it right as Vickie enters the room.

Vickie and Harold exchange a long, deep kiss.

Their love is apparent when Harold thickly says, "Thank you, honey. It was a wonderful birthday."

He picks up his clothes and says he's going to shower, but turns to me before he leaves. "Miranda, I won't forget this. Thank you."

I know I won't forget it either, and watching him mow the lawn next weekend will be extra spicy. After he's gone, Vickie walks with me to the front door.

As I'm leaving, she grabs my arm to stop me. "Our anniversary is in two weeks. He also likes to watch me being fucked by other men. Will you think about it?"

She doesn't give me time to answer when she closes the door. I stand there, dumbly, staring at it for a few seconds. My head is spinning. Did she just ask if I'll let my husband fuck her while Harold watches? I also realize my shoes are still inside their house. I gingerly pick my way across the lawn, cursing every time I step on a pebble.

The idea of Jon fucking Vickie while Harold watches is arousing, but I'm going to need to give this some thought. A LOT more thought.

The End

# ALEC'S HOTWIFE BIRTHDAY

# CHAPTER 1

Today started like any normal Thursday in my hotwife life since I began fucking my four lawyer bosses. It's 8 AM, and my work shift started 30 minutes ago, but I was told to report to Mr. Knight's office for a meeting. My mind air-quotes the word "meeting" because every time I'm alone with one of my bosses, I end up on a desk, bent over a chair, or pressed up against a wall. Mr. Knight—my favorite—is the lawyer who likes bondage, so I'm hoping this involves a silk rope.

My stomach flips as I approach his door, and my pussy buzzes with her approval of this surprise meeting. I call his office The Dungeon because it's in the back corner of the building and decorated in dark wood. And while it might be a joke, I can easily imagine him having an actual dungeon at his house. Instead of knocking, I take a moment to adjust my clothing, compose myself, and press a hand against my belly to calm the butterflies.

My long brown hair is up in a bun, and I check the tension of the topknot to make sure it isn't coming loose. If he fucks me hard enough to mess it up, I might have to wear my hair down for the rest of the day. My fingers trace the outline of the sterling silver kitten necklace I've taken to wearing every day at work, hoping Mr. Knight will call me "Kitten" when he sees me with it on. He often does.

Every time I'm alone with Mr. Knight, my attraction to him grows. It's not healthy for me, but I can't stop thinking about him. The effect he has on me is difficult to explain. Whenever I'm around him, I only want to please him and hear him call me a good girl. I tell myself it's because the sex with Mr. Knight is the best I've had, but, in my more honest moments, I admit that isn't true. I'm half in love with him, and if I ever revealed that to my husband, Jonathan, he would probably insist we stop our hotwife agreement.

My soft knock on the door gets the customary annoyed-sounding "Enter" from Mr. Knight, as if I'm bugging him and he didn't request this meeting. I glance down the hallway to make sure Cindy, the receptionist, isn't lurking close by before I open the door. I don't want her to know how much time I spend alone with the lawyers, so I'm careful whenever I visit one of them. Cindy rarely has any reason to traverse the back hallway, so I'm usually safe when I visit Mr. Knight.

Mr. Knight clacks away on his laptop and doesn't look at me or even stop typing. Part of me thinks he gets off on trying to make me believe he's indifferent, but I'm learning his tells and know it isn't true. Sometimes he's flushed when he meets my gaze, and I've seen him swallow audibly or flare his nostrils. Our attraction to each other is the elephant in the room that I'm content to avoid talking about, since it might ruin everything.

I pause in the middle of his office and clasp my hands in front of me. This is a game we always play, and it may be a few seconds or a few minutes before he acknowledges me. The longer I stand here, the more turned on I become, which is probably the point. I didn't wear panties to work today, intending to torture my husband with up-the-skirt pussy pictures at lunchtime, but now I'm slightly regretting my choice. I fight the urge to rub my legs together, because

I can feel a growing wetness on my inner thigh. Why won't he look at me?

The clock on the wall tells me five minutes have gone by, and he's still typing away, ignoring me. The butterflies in my stomach grow to a slight quiver throughout my body. God, this better end up with me on his desk and his cock inside of me soon. I'm not sure how much longer I can wait, but an invisible force stops me from complaining. I always stay silent until he speaks first.

When he finally glances at me, I'm almost a puddle of desire and I want to drop to my knees in submission. He still doesn't speak. Instead, he circles his desk to stand in front of me. Trembling, I sink to the floor.

"Kitten, don't tempt me. I have a different offer to make."

*What? He didn't bring me in here to fuck?* Breathless, I wait for him to continue while my mind scatters in five different directions. What sort of offer could he have?

"I have a friend, Alec, coming to town, and I think he would enjoy seeing you on your knees."

My brain turns to mush, and I glance up at him with wide eyes and part my lips. I'm unsure how I feel about him wanting to share me, but I'm intrigued. If the all-over body tingle is any sign, I'm also turned on by the idea.

"Why?" I ask quietly.

Mr. Knight caresses my cheek before answering and grins. "Alec is a friend from college, and you are exactly his type. He's visiting the U.S. for his birthday, and you once said you have a fondness for birthdays."

The twinkle in his eyes tells me he remembers a brief conversation where I told him about being my neighbor's birthday gift. He's right—that was a fun day. And despite my concerns afterwards, it didn't turn awkward with the neighbor. Settling more into this idea after being reminded how much I enjoyed the last birthday, I'm curious about Alec.

"Where is Alec from?"

Mr. Knight helps me to my feet and perches on the edge of his desk. "He's living in England now, but he's originally from Scotland."

My pussy perks up, and a jolt of sexual energy zings from my core. Oh, hell yes! He should have led with that. I don't outright broadcast it to anyone, but I have a voice kink and accents get me super hot. Fucking a Scottish dude? Sign me up. My eyes glaze over as I imagine a version of the movie *Braveheart* with me as the heroine, only this one with a happy ending where I don't die.

Mr. Knight snaps his fingers in front of my face, and I jolt. "What?"

He just snickers, and I narrow my eyes at him.

"Is there anything else you need, *Sir*?"

I can't help but get sassy with him since he obviously doesn't plan to fuck me. Besides, I've got work to do while I daydream about a Scotsman in a kilt.

"Not today. Alec will be in town in two weeks. I'll talk with him and let you know what he says."

I turn to leave and put a little extra swing to my hips. If he's watching, he gets a nice ass shake to see what he is turning down.

"Oh, Miranda?"

Pausing, I glance over my shoulder and raise an eyebrow at him.

"I think you're going to have fun with Alec, or I wouldn't suggest this otherwise. Trust me?"

Instead of replying, I blow him a kiss. Two weeks is too far away.

# CHAPTER 2

I was wrong, and the two weeks fly by. Jonathan is all on board for me to fuck a Scotsman. He even watched some *Outlander* episodes with me to get in the spirit. I didn't have the heart to tell him I'm sure Alec is nothing like the hot actors in *Outlander*, but I'm down for whatever is going to make him feel good about the upcoming birthday plans.

Alec is staying at a friend's empty house while they're off touring Europe, so this won't be an awkward hotel hookup. Something about meeting someone I've never met in a hotel doesn't sit right with me, plus this will be the first time I'm going to fuck someone I don't know beforehand.

I'm supposed to be at Alec's house at 6 PM on Saturday. The Wednesday before, Mr. Knight forwards me an email from Alec, along with a picture of him. I devour the picture before reading the contents of the email. Alec is around Mr. Knight's age, so probably mid-to-late 40s. His hair is almost totally grey, which gives me a nice zing since I find older guys sexy. Nothing is really too remarkable about him, but he's an attractive man that I have zero problems picturing myself fucking. The friendly smile on his face helps put me at ease. Since he's Mr. Knight's friend, I wasn't sure what to expect, since Mr. Knight isn't the sociable type.

When I open the email, I'm surprised at the length of it. I was expecting a quick introduction and a general "excited to meet you." The first paragraph includes that information, but the following section gives me pause. The email contains a contract of some type. It has several sections that include: safe words, soft limits, hard limits, expectations, roles, language and praising, and a promise of discretion.

*Uh, what the fuck?* I stare blankly at the message for a full minute while my brain refuses to comprehend anything. I shake my head to clear it. My hands tremble and my heart pounds while I skim the contract. He wants to play from 6 to 9 PM on Saturday and asks that I read over the contract and submit it back to him by email on Friday so that he can review it before I come over. Each section lists items for me to check that I'm willing to do, then some fill-in sections for safe words, and a signature at the bottom as my promise of discretion.

I forward the email to my personal address so I can print it out at home and share it with Jon. Sneaking glances down the hall to make sure I'm still alone, I breathe a sigh and settle in to read it when I'm certain no one is approaching my desk. A gush of wetness floods my panties as I realize Mr. Knight saw this when he forwarded it. Clearly he knows what his friend likes sexually. Guess he thought since I enjoyed being tied up, I'd like a full BDSM experience as well? My body buzzes with tension, and I smirk. He's probably not wrong.

The skin on the back of my neck prickles as I read through the list, but then relaxes slightly when I see a notation at the bottom saying that since this is a onetime play session, I do not have to obey his every command. Alec explains that he only wants to provide some clear guidance on what we both can expect, with nothing set in stone. I can always say no at any point even if I don't say so in the returned contract.

Many of the items on the list sound entertaining. I already know I'm down for spanking and bondage, though it asks me how hard I like to be spanked, and I'm not sure about that answer. I'm willing to go with hard. How much will it really hurt? An ache in my pussy forces me to wiggle in my seat, trying to soothe it. Feeling less intimidated by the contract, I close the email. This is something I'll go over tonight with Jon at home, and we can have some fun with it. Knowing my sweet man, this will give him plenty of ideas, and he'll be off researching BDSM for the next three nights.

I try to concentrate on work, but my mind keeps wandering to the contract, and the ache between my legs distracts me. The occasional wiggle in my chair isn't satisfying any need. For the first time, I wished I had control over when I fucked the bosses. I'd love to storm into an office, bend over a desk, and demand a hard pounding.

*Fuck it!* After an hour, I give up. My drenched panties are now a problem, and if I don't soothe the twinge in my crotch, I'm going to go insane. Casually strolling to the restroom, I pause and fiddle with my shirt so any observers won't think I was rushing. I'm thankful, once again, that it's a single-person bathroom with a lockable door and no stalls. I've lost count of how many times I've masturbated at work since I've started fucking my bosses. Some days, just seeing one of them in a sexy suit is enough to send me running for privacy.

I've done this so often that I have a favorite position. I pull up my skirt and fumble with my panties. I'm desperate to get a finger inside of me and the wet fabric sticking to my pussy lips slows me down. The blue cotton and lace string bikini is one of my favorite panties, but in my haste I snap one of the strings holding it together. *Fuck it.* I rip the rest off and toss it to the side as I lower myself to the floor. My back is against the wall to give me access to my soaking pussy. I learned my lesson once about sitting on my skirt, after I came so hard I squirted and left a wet spot. Now I take precautions and make sure all important clothing is safe from any possible moisture.

I moan when my fingers slide past my wet lips and brush against my clit. Jesus, I should have just done this 30 minutes ago. My only experience with BDSM is what I do with Mr. Knight, but I've seen enough online to imagine being blindfolded and tied up while a guy with thick fingers rubs my pussy. I moan some more when I add in my other hand, using one to rub my clit while two fingers probe my center.

I don't require any warm-up time, since my pussy's already buzzing. I rub furious circles against my clit while massaging in and around the entrance of my hole. My leg muscles tense, and I arch my back from the wall while a loud groan slips out. I grind into my pussy, desperate for release as the tension builds. The man in my daydream does the same as his sausage fingers stretch me wider than mine can. I lose myself in the fantasy, and my loud moans echo in the small room, but I'm beyond caring.

When I come, the strength of my orgasm bows my back and my legs shake as waves of pleasure run through my body. My pussy quivers against my hand and I slow my rubbing, but don't stop fully, riding the peak as long as possible. *Holy fuck!* I'm panting as the room comes back into focus. I relax my legs straight out in front of me and slump against the wall, contemplating my discarded panties across the room. Which is worse? Sitting in wet underwear for the rest of the day or none at all? Since they're ruined, I don't really have an option, but I might as well glory in my sluttiness. After all, I did just rip off my own panties.

I clean up and leave the bathroom, glancing down the hall away from my desk to make sure no one is around. When I turn toward my desk, I almost jump from fright as I see Mr. Knight standing next to it, waiting for me. Uh oh... did he hear me in there? I feel a blush creep up my neck, and I avoid eye contact as I walk past him and sit down.

I croak out a "Yes, Sir?" and take a sip of water and peek up at him from beneath lowered eyelashes.

He's gazing intensely at me with one corner of his mouth raised, as if attempting not to smile. Oh shit, he totally heard me.

"I'm on my way to a meeting, but you didn't confirm that you got the email I forwarded."

Blah, I should have just replied. I shrug and still avoid looking directly at him.

"Oh, yes, sorry. I got it."

"Kitten?"

A thrill zings through me. Goddammit, he knows how the pet name affects me when he says it. I reluctantly bring my gaze up and almost cringe at how breathy my "yes?" sounds.

"Do you see why I think you will have fun with Alec?"

I didn't think I could blush harder, but my face gets hotter. "Yes, Sir."

Mr. Knight leans towards me, tucks a wayward strand of hair behind my ear, and gives me a slight smile.

"Enjoy Saturday night, Kitten."

As he walks away, I sigh and gaze at his backside. Life would be easier if he didn't make me quiver with need whenever I was around him. I daydream for a moment about what would happen if I wasn't married, but force myself back to work.

As the day progresses, every time I think of the contract waiting in my email, a pulse of adrenaline floods my brain.

Yeah, Mr. Knight knows what I like. Saturday is going to be fun.

# CHAPTER 3

Jon and I have an early dinner together on Saturday, and I'm too distracted to say much. He rambles on about his BDSM research and his plans to dom my ass after he watches more videos on how to do it. I can't concentrate on his words, but I smile as he talks to feign interest.

I was totally right about Jon investigating BDSM, and he's so adorable when he gets on a new kick. Having researched nothing myself, he knows more about BDSM than I do at this point. My knowledge extends to the contract I emailed back to Alec, which included stuff I had never heard of. If it wasn't familiar, I said no to it. Which in hindsight might have been shortsighted of me, but I didn't want to scare myself by looking at anything online. I think it's better to go in with few expectations and see what happens.

After dinner, I take a shower before getting dressed in the outfit Jon has picked out for me. He wanted to be a part of the planning, and it seemed harmless. As I glance at the skintight black leather pants that I'd hidden in the depths of my closet, and the red corset top I bought for a Halloween costume, I'm questioning how wise it was to let him decide. I have to suck in my gut to fasten the pants, and I can barely bend over to buckle the strap of the four-inch platform-heeled sandals he told me to wear. The rhinestones on the sandals really bring everything together, though.

The top is a little more difficult, because it has a long row of fasteners in the back, so I call in Jon to help me. He makes quick work of the hooks and nibbles on my shoulder while he's at it, making me giggle. When I glance in the mirror, I grin at how silly I look. Ugh, what will Alec think when he sees me in this outfit?

I teeter to the front door, and Jon puts a black lace shawl around my shoulders, telling me it'll be chilly tonight. I glance at the lace and wonder what world my husband lives in. This won't protect me from even the slightest breeze. But it's the thought that counts, so I kiss his cheek and tell him I'll text him on my way home.

When I slip into the car, I punch the house address into my phone's GPS and pause before leaving the driveway. I'm slightly sick to my stomach from nerves, yet I know I'm excited since I've been wet and daydreaming about being spanked all morning. I just don't know what to expect. But as long as Alec talks to me in a dreamy Scottish accent, then he can do whatever he wants.

My phone says the drive is 30 minutes, but I swear I blink and I'm parked in the driveway of a sprawling one-story stucco house next to a luxury rental car. I adjust my shawl, slide my cellphone into my purse and clutch it in my hand as I do my best to strut to the door. I want to exude confidence when I meet Alec. The song "You're the One that I Want" from the end of the movie *Grease* pops into my head as I walk down the narrow stone path to the front door, and it helps build me up. In this outfit, I'm totally Sandy.

When I ring the doorbell, I'm bobbing slightly to imaginary music. Alec opens the door, and I freeze with my head bent in a weird side tilt. I straighten up, and heat floods my face.

"Hi!"

*Fuck me and my easy-to-blush self.* Alec says nothing for a moment but smiles at me with a sparkle in his eyes. The overall package he presents is quite attractive. His straight white teeth and deep smile lines around his mouth tells me he's often happy. He's dressed casually in jeans and a green t-shirt with no socks or shoes on. The laid-back attitude makes me wonder what he and Mr. Knight had in common in college.

"Come in, Miranda."

His Scottish accent is adorable, and his simple greeting thrills me. Oh, this is going to be a ton of fun tonight. I could close my eyes and listen to this guy all night, and the tingle in my core ramps up to a nice sizzle.

He steps aside and I walk into a massive earth-tone tiled foyer. I've never been in a house this nice. I want to poke my nose everywhere just to see how the other half lives, but something long and furry laid out on a console table against the wall to my left catches my eye. *Uh, what the fuck is that?* I take a step closer and realize there are several things laid out, including a bottle of lube.

I freeze, and my brain blips out as I focus in on dark blue and silver cat ears. The other items on the table color match and include a decorative collar with a blue gem and a tiny bell, a leash, a leather cuff that might attach to an ankle or a wrist, and a long tail that ends in a butt plug.

*Holy fuck.* My mouth drops open, and my eyes widen as I turn my head towards Alec. He's watching my reaction with that sparkle in his eyes.

"I heard you like being called Kitten. Want to have some fun tonight?"

The room tilts on its axis, and a static humming noise overwhelms me. I glance at the tail, and the shiny silver end of the butt plug reflects the lights from above, as if it's winking at me. All my nerve endings come alive, and a pang of longing zips through my core.

"Yes." I breathe out the word with more longing than I intended to portray. Whatever the fuck this is, I'm down with trying it.

Alec laughs, which comes out more like a giggle, and I'm curious how this guy is going to be dominant. He seems way too jolly to be demanding, but something about him is affecting me in ways I didn't expect. The buzzing in my head isn't clearing, and I have an overwhelming need to do whatever he wants.

"Kitten, strip and let me help you into your gear."

Uh, okay. Guess we're doing it here in the foyer. I squat awkwardly and unbuckle my sandals, stepping out of them and pushing them against the wall. Alec takes my shawl and folds it before laying at the end of the table. I set my purse on top of it while Alec moves in behind me. He's warm against my backside as he pushes my hair to the side and kisses the back of my neck. Mmm, he's hitting all the right notes already, and I shiver.

Alec slowly pops open the fasteners of the corset top, and I hold my breath when his fingers brush my spine. When it drops away, the cool air hardens my nipples, and I want to turn around and press against him to feel the contrast of his shirt against my breasts. As I shimmy out of the skin-tight pants, a sense of the surreal washes over me. I met this guy less than 5 minutes ago and here I am stripping naked for him. This is the new sluttiest thing I've ever done, and I love it.

When I'm fully naked, he turns me around to face him and admires the view.

"Lovely."

Under Alec's approving gaze, a soft tingle flutters through me and boosts my self-confidence. I'm going to rock the ears and tail and be the best kitten ever! He reaches to grab a few items, and I wait patiently as he adorns me with the cat ears and adjusts them, tucking my loose wavy hair behind my ears.

I didn't see the black eyeliner pencil on the table and wasn't expecting him to pull it out, uncap it and attempt to draw on my face. I giggle and tilt back a little before he touches the pencil to my cheek. He cups my chin to force me to hold steady, and I try not to laugh more.

"Stand still, Kitten. You need whiskers."

His sexy accent soothes me, and the giggles subside enough that he's able to brush the stripes on my cheek. This feels utterly ridiculous. Also, *what type of guy is into this sort of thing?* I'm assuming the evening will end in sex, but the contract I signed led me to expect a very different experience tonight.

Alec swivels me around again so my back is to him and tells me to hold my hair up from my neck. He kisses along the hairline behind my ear, and I tremble. He pauses before fastening the collar.

"You okay wearing a pretty collar?"

I hesitate for a moment before answering. Why is he asking me this?

"Yes, I'm fine with it."

When he clasps it around me, I stretch my neck in both directions to adjust to the slight restriction. It's not too tight, but it oddly makes me feel like a pet and the butterflies buzz in my stomach again. I'm almost a puddle on the floor, and we haven't even gotten to the sex part of tonight yet. I'm tempted to back up and rub against him to encourage him to hurry. We only have three hours together, and this dressing ritual is eating up precious time.

"Are you ready for your tail?"

*Oh, the tail.* Somehow in all of this, I didn't focus on it being a butt plug. I've had fingers in my ass many times now, but I hadn't progressed to toys yet.

"Uh... yes?"

My hesitancy makes me want to cringe since it goes against my plans to act like a sex goddess who has done it all. Alec laughs softly, and his hand slides up my back.

"Bend over, Kitten."

*Oh fuck, that's hot.* My penchant for being bent over things and the number of times it's actually happened has trained me to become immediately wet whenever someone tells me to bend over. And said with a Scottish accent? Hell, yes. I'll lean over every single surface in this house for Alec and beg for a second round when we're done.

He applies pressure, and I dip my upper half towards the table. I rest my elbows on the edge with my ass pushed out. I spread my legs to give him a better view. He hums his approval.

Expecting Alec to reach for the lube and tail, I jump when his fingers slide against my wet folds. I moan as he rubs circles against my clit. I lean back against his hand and wiggle my ass a little. Jesus, can we just fuck right now and forget the rest of this? I'll forgo the kitten experience if it gets his cock inside me quicker.

He continues to work my bean for a minute. My head is spinning and tiny spikes of pleasure radiate from my core. I'm lost in sensation and cry out nonsense when he stops.

Alec chuckles and reaches for the lube and tail. He fiddles with them while I close my eyes and rest my head on my forearms. A lubed-up finger running around the opening of my asshole jolts me back to reality. *Oh shit, this is really happening.* He takes a moment to lube me up well, pressing a finger or two inside of me, and I'm torn between squirming from pleasure or groaning. I gasp when he replaces his finger with the cold metal of the butt plug and slowly pushes it in. The pressure and fullness as the plug settles forces a moan from my lips.

Alec tugs gently on the tail, testing to make sure it's firmly in place, and I emit a tiny squeak of delight. *Jesus, I might need to get a butt plug after this.* I've barely had it in me for a minute and I already know sex will be amazing with this thing in. A mental picture of me on all fours with him fucking me from behind with the tail pushed up over my back thrills me. Oh yeah, slutty Miranda is 100 percent into this fantasy.

A firm slap on my ass breaks me out of my fantasy, and I yelp. "Hey!"

I'm not sure why I'm complaining. I love being spanked, and the butt plug gives it an extra spicy zing.

"Stand up, Kitten. We have one last part."

*Oooh, yeah, the leash.* My pretty decorative collar can't be used with one, so I'm uncertain what he plans to do with it. When he picks up the leather cuff from the table and attaches it to my wrist, I realize it has a metal loop for a leash hook. When he's done clipping the leash on the loop, he takes four steps backwards and tugs on his end. I raise my hand and take a step forward instead of fighting against the pull, and he smiles at me.

"Come, Pet. Want to see what you look like?"

He gives a tug and I blurt out, "Yes— " but stop cold. How do I address him? When I don't obey the tug, he pauses and stares at me with a fierce expression.

"Uh, what do I call you?"

All traces of humor have left him. He's intense, and heat spreads through my body as I glance towards the floor, unable to meet his gaze. Where did Mr. Jolly Man go?

"You can use Alec. But if you feel like saying something else, you're welcome to."

Relief washes over me. Thank God he wasn't telling me to call him "Sir." Lately I've been reserving that for Mr. Knight, despite knowing it's wrong on some level.

"Also Kitten, we're about to begin. You said in the contract you wanted to use the stop light system for your safe words, so red and yellow, yes?"

I nod to indicate yes, but he doesn't move.

"I need to hear you say it."

Wanting to get started, I blurt out, "Yes, red and yellow."

"Good girl. Ready?"

I give him a jaunty smile to convey that everything is good.

"Okay, Alec. Lead the way."

# CHAPTER 4

I trail five steps behind him as we head down a hall. We enter a bedroom and when I see the bed my pussy clenches, hoping for a hard fucking, but we pause at a full-length mirror.

"You're a pretty wee thing. Don't you agree?"

My reflection startles as much as it enchants me. *Holy shit, I'm adorable.* This is bizarre. I turn to the side to view the tail and swish my hips to watch it sway. The soft fur tickles the back of my legs, and I giggle at how stupid this is, yet fun. In the mirror I can see Alec standing next to the bed, as far as the leash will reach. I can't help but notice the hard bulge in his jeans. Looks like I'm not the only one enjoying this.

"Enough of that. Get on all fours."

*Wait, what?* When I don't immediately obey he patiently repeats himself.

"I said get on all fours, Kitten."

When I sink to my knees, I'm self-conscious and make sure not to glance back at the mirror.

"Now crawl over here."

Alec gives the leash a small tug, and I move the tethered arm forward. I continue the momentum and creep towards him, pausing at his feet. I can't believe I just crawled to him, but I'm tingling and wet so part of me likes everything I'm doing.

"Good girl. Now get up on the edge of the bed."

The praise gives me a tiny rush, and I eagerly climb up the bed. *Hell, yes! Let the fucking commence.* Settling on the edge with my feet dangling off, I wag my tail at him and expect his hand on my pussy again.

He slaps my ass instead.

Since I wasn't expecting it, the shock makes it sting worse than it should. He doesn't hit me hard, but I gasp from the pain. When he quickly smacks the opposite side with his open palm, I whimper. *Shit, why does this feel so good?* He flips the tail up over my back and alternates sides with a smooth rhythm. I lose count after five slaps on each cheek, and the butt plug makes the torture more exquisite. I'm flushed and moan from the burning ache, yet I know he's going light on me. I might have said I'd take a hard spanking, but I'm glad he's not using more force.

Alec pauses after a couple minutes to glide his fingers over my slick pussy lips and dips one finger inside. I squirm back against him, but he removes his hand and slaps my ass again, causing me to groan. I'm crazy turned on, and I wish he'd just fuck me right now.

All movement behind me stops for a moment, and Alec's voice is gruff as he asks, "Kitten, shall we go play?"

I perk up at the word "play" and glance over my shoulder. He's holding the leash and walking towards the door as if he expects me to follow him. Guess we aren't playing in the handy bedroom WE WERE ALREADY IN!

I scoot off the bed without hesitation and follow him. This is his birthday, so whatever he wants, goes. I'm just along for the ride. But hopefully this ends with a cock inside of me or else I might have to attack Jonathan when I get home. I smirk when I think of my husband. He's going to shit bricks when I tell him about dressing up like a kitten. This possibility wasn't on either of our radars, and he speculated I would be tied up tonight. I should have bet on it, but I thought since Alec was Mr. Knight's friend that bondage would be on the menu as well.

As I follow him through the house, I amuse myself by swinging my hips side-to-side as I walk so that my tail swishes behind me. The butt plug makes my pussy ache, and I'm extra hungry for Alec's cock. But since I just met him, I don't know the best way to get it. He leads me to a large family room with a square brown leather ottoman sitting in the middle with a matching couch against the wall. I barely have time to question the ottoman's odd placement before we're in front of it.

"Get up and kneel for me."

Mr. Knight said Alec would want me to kneel, and he wasn't wrong. I rest my knees on the edge and crawl up. The ottoman is a little awkward, and I can't do it exactly the way Mr. Knight taught me, but I'm able to keep my back straight, with my knees spread apart and my hands on my thighs, palm up. It takes a moment to adjust the tail behind me, and any slight tug on it produces a zing of delight. Alec unhooks the leash and drops it to the floor. He steps back a few paces and tilts his head, studying me.

"Perfect. What a good little kitten you are."

I thrill at being called a "good little kitten" just as much as hearing "good girl," and a calmness invades my mind as I sink deeper into my desire to please. The rest of the world fades away, and I'm completely focused on Alec and this moment with him.

The insides of my thighs are wet, and I resist the urge to grind the butt plug against the ottoman. The bulge in front of his jeans appears larger than it did earlier, and I lick my lips, wishing he'd pull out his cock. If he'd just give me a peek at what he was hiding, then maybe it would satisfy me until he's done playing out whatever scenario is going on in his head. He clearly had this all planned out, so he must have a schedule of sorts. Wonder what would have happened if I said no?

"So, my pet, do you think you deserve a treat?"

*Oooh, here we go!* I vigorously nod and give a firm, "Yes."

*Oh heck yeah, I'm going to ask to see his cock.* At this point I don't care what size it is. A slim marker would get me off.

"Why do you think you deserve a treat?"

*Uh, what the fuck?* Am I supposed to make up something? I wrack my brain for any excuse I can come up with that might sound plausible.

I'm hesitant as I reply. "Because you said I was a good kitten, and I've done everything you've asked?"

Alec seems to think about that for a moment. "This is true, you have. What treat would you like?"

I experience an unexpected rush of energy when he agrees with me, and I realize he's only toying with me. I can get down with this type of mind game. *Fuck, why is this so hot?* My resolve to be the best kitten ever overwhelms me, and I come to a sudden understanding of how to get exactly what I want.

It's time to show him that this kitten can play the game just as well as he can.

I tilt my head at him and relax a little on the ottoman, not sitting at attention any longer, and the shift of the tail produces a nice pleasant pull on the butt plug.

"I'd like to taste your cock. Does my Master need me to beg?"

Alec doesn't respond or move, and I have a moment of self-doubt and wonder if I read the situation wrong. But when he lets out a small, imperceptible breath, I realize he was holding it after my response. I want to cheer as he walks up to me, unzipping his jeans along the way.

When he pulls out his absolute monster of a cock, I can't help but widen my eyes. *Uh, okay. That's no pencil dick.* He's thick with bulging veins, and, as he gets closer, I swear I see it pulsate. He's slightly wet with pre-cum, and I desperately want to taste him. Before he can change his mind or actually make me beg, I open my mouth and stick my tongue out flat. I peer up at him, daring him to resist me.

He guides his cock to my waiting tongue. When I try to reach up to help him, he stops me.

"No hands. Kittens don't have hands."

*Oh, shit.* Okay, we'll play it this way. I keep my hands down as his cock fills my mouth. I'm half afraid he won't fit, but it ends up being fine. Slightly tight, but he's not choking me, so I relax and savor the salty pre-cum mixed with another undefinable flavor that isn't unpleasant. My tongue swirls around his shaft, caressing the veins, and another jolt of power kicks me in the stomach, knowing Alec wasn't able to resist my treat request.

He said I can't help him, but he never said anything about touching myself, so I reach between my legs as he slowly thrusts in and out of my mouth. As soon as my hand reaches my pussy lips, Alec growls at me.

"Did you ask permission to touch yourself?"

*Ugh, fuck.* Quickly removing my hand from between my legs, I stop sucking and look up at him.

He withdraws his cock from my mouth and demands, "Have you something to ask your Master, Kitten?"

Realizing I'm not the one in control of the situation the way I thought, I keep my tone meek.

"Master, may I touch myself while I enjoy my treat?"

Alec contemplates me for a moment, and I glance back at his saliva-coated cock waving in front of my face. I lick my lips while fighting the urge to lean forward and fit my lips around the tip.

"Yes, Kitten. Now open wide."

I'm surprised at the ripple of happiness when Alec agrees, and I part my lips just in time to engulf the tip again as he pushes it towards me. He's being careful, and I appreciate it based on his size. I'm sure once I adjust to him, I can handle it as rough as he wants. But for a first time with him, I like the care he's taking, and it makes me more eager to please him. I want this to be his best birthday ever.

I'm dripping wet, and my finger rubs circles on my clit as I suck on Alec. I don't fully notice when I speed up my hand movement, but the pressure in my core builds. The butt plug, along with the rubbing, pushes me towards an orgasm. Throwing myself enthusiastically onto Alec's cock, I suck harder and try to force him deeper, and I'm rewarded with sharp moans from him that spur me on to sluttier heights.

I'm desperate to come, and I want him to come with me. Spikes of pleasure from my pussy tell me I'm almost there, so I suck on him harder. I moan around him and close my eyes as rapture threatens to overwhelm me.

When he rips his cock from my mouth, I involuntarily mewl a complaint. I open my eyes and pout at him, and stop moving my hand. I give a pathetic little "Why?" Feeling cheated, I can't think of anything else to say.

"Get down on all fours. This is my choice, and you're going to be my fucktoy who does exactly what I want."

*Oh, hell yes!* No one has called me a fucktoy before, and his accent makes everything he says more erotic. Slutty Miranda loves it. Alec has totally switched off his sweet side, and when I'm not quick enough to get down, he roughly pulls me onto the floor, grabs my hair, and shoves my head towards the carpet.

For a moment I think he's pulling out the tail, but he's only grabbing it and pinning it under one of his hands as he seizes my hips and rams his cock straight to my core. He grabs my hair with the hand not holding the tail and pulls it back, forcing my head up.

"Ooooh, fuck!" I moan as his thickness stretches me.

He doesn't give me time to adjust to his size as he drills into me repeatedly, each thrust tugging on the butt plug. Holy shit. I'm being torn apart by his roughness, and his crazed fucking zings all the nerve endings of my pussy to the shattering point. He lets go of my hair to grab my hips with his other hand as well. Instead of fighting his momentum, I stretch my arms out and relax my upper body towards the floor. My fingers encounter the cat ears that must have flown off my head in the roughness. I wrap my fingers around the band and clutch it as he plows into me. His balls slap against my clit, and the angle I'm in makes every thrust hit the perfect spot at my core. My nipples scrape against the carpet and add to the delight coming from my pussy and ass.

Alec growls at me. "You love being my fucktoy, don't you?"

"Yes," I gasp.

"Say it," he growls. "Say you love being my fucktoy."

Oh shit, he actually wants me to repeat it? I can't think properly, and it's hard to form sentences.

"I love being... your... fuck—ooooch."

I almost come as he yanks on my hair and forces my head up from the floor.

"Now say it again, slut, so I can hear it."

I thrill at the command in his voice, and I'm moaning and panting as I try to reply. The exquisite agony from his thrusts and the butt plug spiral me closer and closer to my orgasm.

"I love being your... fucktoy... Master!"

Alec groans behind me. "What a fucking good little kitten you are."

The ping in my brain from being called a good little kitten topples me over the edge, and I scream out as I explode around his cock.

"Oooooh!"

Waves of intense pleasure rock through me, and I buck and shudder against him. I almost peak again when he pulls the butt plug out. He releases my hair so he can grab my hips with his hands. Giving a few final hard thrusts, he unloads ropes of cum deep inside my pussy. He growls loudly, and I'm lost in my world of bliss. My cave walls milk his cock as he spurts everything he has, jerking until he's finally finished.

I'm coming down from my peak still, and tiny spikes of pleasure vibrate up and down my body as he wraps his arms around me. We both sink to the floor on our sides, me as the little spoon. I can feel his cum and our mixed juices running out of me. We're a sweaty mess, but I don't care. It's too nice lying with him while I continue to shudder from slight aftershocks.

# CHAPTER 5

I float in my happy place for an indeterminate amount of time while I enjoy his cum leaking from my pussy. I'm not sure I've ever been more thoroughly fucked, though thinking back on some of the things I said and did makes me blush as the sexual haze fades. Uh, did I really call him "Master?"

I stir slightly as he moves away and the cool air washes over my newly exposed moist skin, but my eyes are closed and I'm too drained to open them. He's gone for a moment, but when he returns, he sits down and slips his arms under my side. He kneels and pulls me up into his lap as he leans against the couch, cradling me.

"Kitten, look at me."

Alec's voice is again soothing and soft, and I snuggle closer to him, not obeying his command. He smells like sex and sandalwood, and it's comforting. His fingers brush against my cheek and across my lip.

"Kitten, open your eyes. You need to take a sip of water."

The mention of water stirs me, and I crack my eyelids to see an open bottle of water in front of my face. I grab it from him and take a sip, the cold water waking me up a bit more.

"Atta girl. Now open up and take a bite of a cracker."

I open my mouth like a baby bird. I could have fed myself, but when he puts a cracker in my mouth, I enjoy the feeling of being taken care of. As I munch, I feel more like myself. But the longer I sit there, the more images of what we did flood over me and I want to hide against his chest.

I let some dude use a leash on me?

I'm tempted to ask him if he had fun, but I'm too uncertain about what happened and afraid that if I ask him, he'll ask me the same question.

"Miranda, are you okay?"

Alec using my name helps, and I nod against his chest and give a small yes. We sit for a long time, and eventually I shiver a little. I've never reacted to sex like this before. He rubs my back and strokes my hair while I'm melted against him, feeling totally safe in his arms. He continues to feed me bites of crackers and makes sure I take sips of water every once in a while. After what feels like forever, I'm relaxed and my mind clears enough to hold a conversation.

"Alec, did you have fun?"

He chuckles against my hair.

"Oh, yes, Miranda. That was amazing. Thank you for a wonderful night."

A warm glow washes over me, and I can tell by the tone of his sexy voice that he really enjoyed it. The tail and cat ears scattered across the floor catch my eye, and I giggle. I reach up and finger the collar.

"Alec, may I keep the collar?"

He squeezes me tighter against him.

"Of course."

I smile against his chest, glad to have a token from tonight.

"Do you want to talk about anything?" he asks.

When he asks this question, I realize I don't need to right now. I want some time to process. As my head clears, I know that tonight was fabulous and that I will be okay. Plus, only he and I know what we did. I'm not sure yet how much I plan on telling Jon. I plan to give it some thought on the drive home.

As if reading my mind, Alec interrupts my thoughts.

"I'm driving you home. You can get your car tomorrow."

His commanding tone leaves no room for argument, and I'm too content to argue. We both stand up, and he shows me to the bathroom and brings me my clothes. I regard my wild hair and smudged kitten whiskers in the mirror, then smile as I wash my face and smooth my hair. I'm tired and don't want to get dressed in my slut outfit again, but left with nothing else to wear, I have no choice.

When I venture out to find Alec, I'm clutching the corset to my chest since I need help to fasten it in the back. I find him in the family room. He helps me finish dressing, then hands me a pair of slippers instead of my shoes. I look at him quizzically.

"I don't want you to fall and hurt yourself. Wear them until we get to your house."

Grateful to not have to teeter around in those towering heels, I put on the slippers. We're soon ensconced in his car and heading back toward my house. I text Jon that I'm on my way home and that Alec is driving me. Jon replies that he'll be waiting.

The drive is mostly quiet but pleasant. We listen to music while I doze lightly. When we pull into the driveway, I see Jon looking out the front window. Before I get out of the car, Alec takes my hand, kisses it, and hands me a business card.

"Thank you for a lovely evening, Miranda. If you want to talk about anything, call me. The card has my personal cell number on it."

His offer of talking warms me. I slip his card in my purse and smile at him as I climb out. I stop to remove the slippers, toss them onto the passenger seat, and grab my sandals.

"Thank you, Alec. Happy birthday."

I turn towards home as the front door opens and Jon comes out to greet me, engulfing me in a hug. We both watch Alec drive away.

A pang hits me when I realize I will probably never see Alec again. But Jon's arms around me feel right, and I'm where I belong. As we walk into the house together, I know this was a night I will never forget.

The End

# JON'S HOTWIFE BIRTHDAY

# CHAPTER 1

I'm in lust with a woman for the first time. My eyes follow our server, Danielle, as she moves around the restaurant. God, she's hot. My best friend, Dina, brought me here a month ago, and I'd never been before. Danielle was the server that night too, and my entire body tingled whenever she came to our table.

To see if it would happen again—you know, for science—I visited the next week with my husband, Jon, on the same weekday and time, and she was working again. I requested her section, and when she greeted me with a friendly smile and said it was nice to see me again, the butterflies kicked in and I knew it was lust. Since then, I've been eating at the restaurant twice per week and I always request her table. Jon assumes this is my new favorite place because of the food and I've yet to tell him otherwise.

"So what do you think?" Jon's voice startled me out of my reverie.

"Uh, what? Sorry, I was distracted."

Jon snickers as he chews on a French fry.

"I saw you watching Danielle. Do you think she's pretty?"

Oh, my sweet boy, 'pretty' does not describe my thoughts of Danielle. But I keep that to myself.

"I think she's beautiful. Don't you?"

Jon contemplates Danielle's backside while she's leaning over a table to clean it, and a zing of electricity shoots through my pussy. I squirm in my seat a little. Why is this so hot? I want Jon to say she's gorgeous so I can ask him if he would "do" her. I'd watch Jon and Danielle together if they made a porno. Jon's sandy-blonde hair and boyish charm, along with Danielle's long dark hair and sexy curves... mmm, yeah, that visual gets me wet.

Jon clears his throat and sips his water before answering. "She has appeal."

I want to laugh at Jon. Appeal, my ass. He knows she's hot, but he's probably afraid I'll get jealous.

Jon munches another fry before directing the conversation back to what he was trying to say before. "Hey, stop changing the subject. Do you have any thoughts about what we should do for my birthday?"

Oh shit, that's what he was asking me while I was drooling over Danielle. His birthday falls on a Tuesday this year, which is an odd day on which to celebrate, but we could at least do dinner and a movie. I'm about to suggest that idea when Danielle appears at our table.

"Are you guys doing good? Do you want anything else?"

Shit, even Danielle's voice is hot. She has a light feminine voice that is oh-so-sexy. Can I order a side of her to go? My brain freezes, and I don't reply while Jon tells her we don't need anything. Danielle smiles directly at me, and I swear she winks before she says she'll be right back with our check. My eyes follow her and a kinky idea pops into my head.

"Jon, we should have a threesome."

Jon chokes on a fry and has to take a drink before replying. "For my birthday?"

Oooh, his dang birthday again. I was plotting the threesome for any time, but this is a good excuse.

"Yeah, for your birthday."

I'm still watching Danielle as I contemplate the threesome idea. Too bad I don't know her that well. I'd love to invite her to the private party.

"What girl would want to join us? Do you have someone in mind?"

I glance sharply at Jon, finding it curious that he didn't give me an immediate no. Several months ago we opened our marriage so I could play with other people in a hotwife situation. Jon expressed no desire to fuck anyone else, and I assumed he was happy with the way things were going. He always gets gloriously possessive when I come home and tell him about my sexual escapades. Our sex life is better than ever and neither of us wants to end the hotwife agreement.

I shrug. "No, I don't know anyone. It was only a thought."

Only a dirty, slutty daydream that included our server, but that's my fantasy life. My life in the real world means I have no one to ask to be our third. Jon laughs at me and all conversation about a threesome ends.

Jon gets up to use the restroom before we leave. While he's gone, Danielle brings the bill over. When she sets it on the table, I notice her long slender fingers end with red painted nails, and I wonder if she paints her toes to match.

"It was nice seeing you, Miranda. Hope to see you again next week."

Oh shit, she knows my name? I'm the one who always signs the receipt and I give her generous tips, but I didn't know she paid attention.

Danielle turns to leave when I stop her. "Hey, Danielle. Do you work on Tuesdays?"

She looks slightly puzzled when she replies. "No, it's my day off. Why?"

My bravado fails me and I can't proposition her. "I was considering coming here for Jon's birthday next week and you're our favorite server so I was just curious."

"Oh, thanks! Hope you guys enjoy his birthday."

I let out a whoosh of air when she leaves. God, I'm such an idiot. I write in a large tip and sign my name and slide the pen and receipt across the table when an idea hits me. Snatching the paper, I flip it over and then glance in the direction of the bathroom to see if Jon is coming back yet. When I don't spot him, I scribble a note on the back of it.

*I'm looking to make my husband's birthday special. Text me if you are interested.*

I leave my phone number, and then turn the receipt over and under the tip portion I write, "See back."

I jump when Jon returns. "Ready to go?"

"Uh, yes!" I want to run away from the table as quickly as possible. What the fuck was I thinking? I resist the urge to take the receipt and crumple it up, but how would I explain it got ruined?

Jon puts his arm around me and we walk through the restaurant side by side. I can't help but peek behind me and I see Danielle pick up the receipt off the table and glance at the back of it. Her head jerks up and our eyes meet, but her expression is unreadable from this distance. I flash a smile at her and turn my attention forward before I trip on something.

Yep, pretty sure I can never come to this restaurant again.

# CHAPTER 2

The next two days are agony, and I mentally berate myself for ruining our ability to eat at the restaurant again. Jon wants to know if we're going there on Friday for our date night and I tell him it might be time to try somewhere new for a change. Work is a grind because my bosses are all in Vegas for a conference. I'm sure it's just an excuse to travel and party, but that means I'm not being fucked at work this week and my pussy is not happy. I've grown used to being taken in various locations around the office, sometimes randomly, and it makes work fly by.

On the third day after my embarrassing debacle with Danielle, I'm relaxing in the break room when my phone chirps that I have a text message. Swiping it open, I assume it will be from Jon, but it's an unknown number.

*This is Danielle, and I'm interested. What did you have in mind?*

Holy shit. I drop my phone on the break room table and stare at it with wide eyes. What do I say back? My hands are shaking when I pick it back up, and a gush of wetness hits my panties. I was not expecting this at all. I try to calm my nerves as I type my reply.

*Jon wants a threesome for his birthday, and*
*we both think you are sexy. I know this is*
*crazy, but do you want to join us?*

My brain buzzes when I press send on the message. I swear every few weeks I keep telling myself I just did the most slutty thing I've ever done in my life, and again this one takes the cake. I just propositioned some random server I barely know.

Reaching down, I slip a hand under my skirt and rub my pussy through my panties while I wait for Danielle to reply. She may not even respond, but the thought of licking her delicious skin is more than I can handle. This is Jon's birthday, but I came up with the idea and I want to partake in the fun. I've never been with a woman before, but the sexual exploration after becoming a hotwife has driven me to explore areas I never imagined I would. I've been fucking my bosses and been a random birthday gift to a couple of guys. Fucking my husband and another woman at the same time seems tame compared to things I've done in the recent past.

I'm getting myself worked up with my hand, and right when I'm contemplating moving to the bathroom to take things further, my phone dings with a text from Danielle. Using my free hand, I swipe the screen to read it.

*Sounds fun to me. Text me the details.*

Ooooh, hell yes! As soon as I finish reading the message, I slip my hand underneath my panties and press two fingers into my slick cave. Cindy, the receptionist, could walk into the break room at any moment but I don't care. I finger fuck myself thinking of Danielle and wishing it was her pussy I was playing with. I don't know where this newfound interest in a woman came from, but it's hot and I'm going with it.

Leaning back in the chair, I spread my thighs wider and pull my skirt up so I can get a deeper thrust with my fingers. I add in my second hand, rubbing my clit at the same time. My soft moans echo a little in the room, but I'm beyond caring. I need release, and my legs tense as the pleasure builds.

I'm about to come when I hear Cindy close outside in the hall, talking loudly to the paralegal. "I think we have extra in the break room. I'll look."

Fuck! I pull my wet fingers from my pussy and slide my skirt down as best as I can while Cindy strolls in.

"Oh, hey Miranda. Thought you left for lunch."

I'm fuzzy and in a sexual daze so I stumble on my reply. "Uh, no—no, just eating here."

Cindy nabs some paper towels from a cupboard above the sink and smiles at me as she leaves. A few seconds later she comes back in.

"Oh, forgot more water!" She fills up her reusable bottle from the water fountain and strolls out again.

Jesus, that was too close. I get up and wash my juices off my hands at the sink before packing up my lunch. I'm so wet and turned on. Back at my desk I text my husband.

*You better be ready to fuck me when you get home tonight.*

I try to work after he replies with an emoji eggplant and fireworks. Guess this means he's down for some fun. It's going to be a long afternoon of frustration until then.

# CHAPTER 3

As soon as I walk in the door after work, my phone pings; it's a text message from Jon.

*I want you naked and kneeling in the kitchen when I get home tonight.*

Oh, holy fuck. What is this? My pussy clenches and I fight the urge to rub away the ache that's been building since Cindy interrupted me in the break room earlier. Jon has been doing extensive BDSM research ever since I was the birthday gift for a super hot Scottish guy named Alec, but Jon never asked me to kneel for him before, nor has he tried any sort of control over me. This is a new development.

Knowing my husband won't be home for a couple of hours is horrible. I'm tempted to snag my dildo and go to town, but I know it will make whatever Jon does ten times hotter if I wait. What is he going to do to me when he gets home? He better not be expecting just a blow job. I need that man's cock inside me in a bad way. My text message said to fuck me tonight and I couldn't have been more clear. But why did he ask me to kneel?

When Jon gets home, I've worked myself up to the point I'm practically vibrating as I kneel on the linoleum kitchen floor. I'm flushed, wet, and my nipples pucker in the cool air. I don't know what to expect. Does Jon want me looking down, or can I look at him in the face? This stunt of his is probably the most erotic thing he's done to me in months.

Jon passes by the kitchen and doesn't say hello. *Uh, what the fuck*? I hear him rustling around in the master bathroom. I'm too curious to keep my gaze down, and I'm glancing at the kitchen doorway when he enters, fully naked and erect.

*Oooh, hello*. I smile at him in greeting.

"I've been waiting here patiently like you told me."

I crave to add that I'm a good girl, but I'm uncertain how Jon will react. Something about kneeling and waiting for him lulls me into a mood where I wish to please him. I'd do whatever he wants right now, and the thought of only sucking on his cock holds more appeal than before.

Jon stands back for a moment, observing me, and I squirm a little. I'm so wet, the moisture is running down my crease, and I'm probably leaving a puddle on the floor. What is he waiting for?

After another few seconds, I've reached my limit and have to ask, "So, my love, what do you want me to do?"

Jon approaches me and holds out his hands for me to grab. He helps me up before answering.

"You're going to bend over the kitchen table so I can fuck you like you asked."

I'm enjoying this facet of Jon and quickly obey. I move the chair away from the end and fold over the edge of the table, resting my face on the cool surface and gripping the sides with my hands. Jon immediately moves behind me, pressing the head of his cock against my aching hole.

I grip the sides tighter as he slips into me, slowly, inch by glorious inch. I moan and shove back against him, forcing him in fully. Taking his time, he slides his hands to my hips and fucks me deep. With each thrust he bottoms out and gives an extra hard push as if he's reminding me that slow doesn't mean soft. Zings of delight radiate from my core. My moans quickly turn into loud chanting of "Oh, my god," and enthusiastic groans.

Jon picks up the pace and hammers into me while my mind goes blank from the pleasure. He moves his hands from my hips, grasping the table to use as leverage to fuck me harder. I'm not sure he's ever been this demanding, and it thrills me.

Jon is less verbal than usual and the only sound coming from him is harsh panting and the noise of our sweaty flesh slapping together. The table makes a tiny squeak with each thrust, but I'm beyond caring. The zings of pleasure intensify and when I close my eyes, stars light up behind them. Pressure in my core builds and I'm rushing towards my orgasm and I can tell Jon is close as well.

When I replace my cries of "Oh, god" with a plea for Jon to fuck me harder, he bucks wildly, and it pushes me over the abyss. My entire body shakes with the force of my orgasm as pleasure washes over me. My pussy clenches and spasms against his rod when he explodes with a loud groan. He halts his movement while he's fully inside, and he quivers against me and pumps his hot cum deep in me.

He relaxes against me as I come down from my high, and we're both sticky with sweat. I finally let go of the table and he wraps his arms around me and slides us carefully to the hard kitchen floor, cushioning me so I'm snuggled on top of him and not on the cold linoleum.

Floating, content, in my happy place, I'm a limp noodle. I don't know what got into Jon tonight, but I wouldn't mind if this side of him came out more often. I could try just being naked and kneeling when he gets home from work occasionally to surprise him and see what happens.

Jon's voice rumbles through his chest. "Was that good or what?"

Knowing I need to give him positive reinforcement because I want more of this, I giggle. "Yeah, that was fabulous."

Jon sighs in contentment and it's a while before either of us gets up.

# CHAPTER 4

By the time Jon's birthday comes around, I'm a nervous wreck. All weekend I vacillated between crazy horny and freaked out whenever I thought of the upcoming plans. The best part is that I didn't tell Jon anything. He has zero clue that Danielle will be at the house when he gets off work tonight.

Danielle and I have been constantly texting about the plan. She received some sexy lingerie as a gift for her recent birthday that she thinks Jon will love, and when she snapped a selfie in the provocative red ensemble, I realized I needed to up my game. I went on a secret shopping spree and bought a seductive black bustier and new thigh-highs that will drive him wild. His mind is going to be blown tonight. He thinks we're just going to dinner and then making an early night of it, but I hinted that he might get lucky, to make sure he was in the mood. So far it's working, since he keeps texting with lewd emojis and comments.

The odd thought that kept running through my mind all weekend was where to have the threesome. We don't have a spare room with a large bed, so the obvious place would be the master bedroom. But do I want to bring someone else literally into my bed? I decide to have

Danielle wait in the bedroom, and when it's time for the surprise, I'll go in and get her and bring her out to the living room.

This might be Jon's birthday, but the thought of running my hands up Danielle's legs and kissing her inner thighs is keeping me at a high state of arousal, and I'm incredibly wet.  I'm more sexually open after a few months of being a hotwife, and with how hot I am for her, you'd never know I hadn't been with a woman before. I'm enjoying the erotic freedom and my fantasies include things I never previously considered.

After work, I rush to the store to pick up Jon's birthday cake and a few other supplies. I need to get back to the house before Danielle arrives. I'm pulling into the driveway right as she's walking down the sidewalk from the neighbor's house. We live on a quiet street and an unfamiliar car parked out front would stand out, so I arranged for her to park next door.

I wave a greeting to her and when I get out of the car, she gives me a hug. The light floral scent of her perfume and the soft skin on her arms makes my head spin. I've never hugged a woman knowing that in an hour I would be doing a lot more than just casually touching her.

I grin at her. "Thank you for doing this. Jon is going to love it."

Danielle only smiles back in reply, tucks the strap of the bag she brought with her over her shoulder, and helps me carry a couple bags of groceries inside. As I unpack the supplies, I make idle chitchat, and I can tell we're both uneasy. As I ramble on about nothing in particular, she's nodding her head and making correct responses, but we're fluttering around with nervous energy.

Knowing Jon won't be home for an hour, I stop what I'm doing and pull out two shot glasses and a bottle of Jose Cuervo tequila. I'm not usually a shot-taking type of woman, but my level of nervousness requires alcohol, fast.

"I think we need to relax."

"I agree," Danielle laughs and sits down at the bar stool at the kitchen counter while I cut up a lime I bought at the store and slide the salt shaker to her.

Together we lick the back of our hands and shake salt on them. We smile at each other before licking the salt, draining the shot glasses, and snagging a wedge of lime to suck on. I shudder from the harsh alcohol and I'm reminded why I don't do shots often. Danielle seems to have fared better with the shot, so maybe she samples it occasionally since she works in a restaurant with a bar. For two people who are about to sleep together, we haven't shared too many details about our lives. She could be a party girl for all I know.

We chatter for another fifteen minutes until the alcohol hits us. We're giggly and relaxed, and the longer I'm close to her, the more turned on I'm getting. She's wearing a pink V-neck t-shirt and I want to kiss the hollow of her neck below her ear. Maybe Jon will just watch and I can play with Danielle all night? This thought doesn't displease me.

Glancing at the clock, I quickly clean up the tequila supplies and hide them.

"We should get ready in case he comes home early."

Jon rarely does get off work early, but today would be the day it could happen—especially since I'm still getting random raunchy text messages from him, so I know he's in the mood for some birthday sex. Danielle follows me into the master bedroom, sets her bag on the bed, and removes the sexy red lingerie she modeled for me in the selfie.

When she sweeps her shirt off over her head to expose a pink bra, my brain freezes. Oh, shit. This is really happening. I've been fantasizing about Danielle all week, and the moment is finally here. Not wanting to look like I'm ogling her, I head into my walk-in closet to dig for my hidden new purchase. To give her some privacy, I strip and change in the closet.

I keep a chair in the there and I prop my foot up on it, smoothing the last thigh-high up my leg, when Danielle peeks through the doorway. She leans against the doorframe in her red lingerie, and my mouth goes dry. The bright lights leave little to the imagination, and I can see almost everything through the sheer fabric. I love everything about Danielle's body. She's got curves in all the right places and I want to reach out and run my fingers through her hair to feel if it's as soft as it looks.

Realizing Danielle is looking at my leg propped on the chair, I bring it down to the floor and we both take a step towards each other at the same time. She's taller than I am, but not by much, and feeling brave in the moment, I reach up and caress her cheek. She leans into my hand slightly, and taking that as a positive sign, I press against her and stand on tiptoe to brush my lips softly against hers.

She brings her head down and when the kiss deepens, spikes of pleasure shoot straight to my pussy. I'm tempted to slip my hands between her legs to see if she's as wet as I am, but I don't want Jon to get home and find us fucking without him. I'm not sure I could stop myself once my finger is inside her. And yet, I'm afraid I'm already at the point where I can't stop as I run my thumbs over the cup of her bra and flick her puckered nipple through the fabric.

I pull my lips from hers and nibble down her neck, pausing at the spot below her ear I wanted to kiss earlier. My entire body is zinging with need, and I want to push her backwards into the bedroom and onto the bed to ravish her. I'm about to act on my spontaneous thought when Jon calls out.

"Hey, I'm home. Where are you at?"

Oh, shit. Danielle and I freeze, look at each other with wide eyes, and then giggle.

"Here, hide in the closet. I'll come get you in a minute." I partially close the door to the closet and head out of the bedroom.

# CHAPTER 5

I meet up with Jon in the hallway.

"Oh, wow. Hi!" Jon looks pleased at the black corset, lace bikini panties, and thigh-highs.

I run my arm up the wall and pose in my awkward, sexy way, and purr at him. "Happy birthday, Jon. Want to play tonight?"

"Mmm, Kitten, you know I do. I've been thinking about you all day."

Jon moves towards me and claims a passionate kiss that leaves me breathless when he breaks it off.

"Do you mind if I shower first?"

Ugh. I hadn't considered that he would want to shower, and that he might get clean clothes from the closet.

"Go for it. Why don't I grab you something relaxing to wear when you get out?"

He gives me a quick, "Thanks Kitten," and a kiss on my forehead before heading into the master bathroom. When I enter the closet, Danielle is lounging on the chair. I make a snap decision to just use the master bed for the festivities, despite being uncertain earlier.

"He's taking a shower. I think we should both be on the bed when he gets out."

Danielle giggles at the idea and we both stretch out on our sides, facing the doorway. Her head is up by the headboard, but I position mine opposite, so I'm down towards the end of the bed, closer to the door, and can see out in the hallway. Danielle tickles the bottom of my stocking-clad feet and I stifle a laugh and shift my legs to a safer location.

Jon doesn't take long and when he leaves the bathroom, he only has a towel around his waist. He whistles at me when he enters the bedroom, expecting to find clothes laid out for him and freezes when he notices Danielle.

"So, Jon, I guess I didn't mention we had a guest. Danielle wants to help us celebrate your birthday."

I smile at his shocked expression, and I can tell he doesn't know how to answer.

I can't help teasing him. "Is it okay if she joins in the fun?"

That seems to shake him out of his stupor. "Oh, hell yes!"

His enthusiastic reply makes me giggle, and I climb off the bed.

"Why don't you just sit down then, Mr. Birthday Boy."

I push him towards the bed and he perches on the edge, while I go into the closet and grab the chair. I position it a few feet in front of him and sit down. Jon looks slightly bewildered and Danielle hasn't moved. I sigh inwardly, knowing that I'm going to need to take charge because Jon won't.

"Jon, lie on your back on the bed."

When he immediately does what I say, a slight buzz hits my head. Well, that was nice. I stand up and walk over to him, lean down, and kiss him deeply. He still has the towel around his waist and I rub his cock through the damp cotton. He grows harder in my hand and when I tug at the towel, he lifts his hips up off the bed so I can pull it out from under him. I break off the kiss and nibble down his chest, heading towards his erect member jutting straight up in all its glory.

I stroke him slowly and glance over at Danielle. She's playing with her nipples through the fabric of her lingerie bra, and I want her to have some fun as well.

I command her softly. "Danielle, come over here and kiss Jon."

She slides across the bed and I watch the two kissing for a moment before taking Jon's throbbing cock in my mouth. He groans and his member pulsates against my tongue; I taste his salty pre-cum and lick at it eagerly. He shifts his upper body so I can suck on him while he plays with Danielle's breasts and continues to ravage her mouth.

Well, this is fucking hot, but I don't want Jon to get too excited too fast. I stop sucking on him and remove his cock from my mouth with an audible pop. Sitting back in the chair, I'm enjoying the show while Jon rolls on his side towards Danielle to focus more attention on her. When he brushes his lips down her neck and begins to remove her lingerie bra, a surging buzz in my brain hits me.

"Hey, stop." My voice is firm, with no trace of amusement.

Jon freezes and peers over his shoulder at me.

"Did you ask if you could take that off?"

Hearing the words come out of my mouth, I'm reminded of Alec's birthday and how he made me ask permission to touch myself. Being the one in control is pretty fun.

Jon is hesitant when he answers. "Uh, no?"

"That's right, you didn't. Do you have something to ask me?"

The glint in Jon's eye tells me he's getting worked up by what I'm doing.

"Uh, Kitten, can I take off Danielle's bra?"

What's this? Kitten doesn't give orders. I make a quick decision on the fly.

"No, ask again. This time do it properly and call me Mistress."

"Oh," Jon exhales sharply, and I swear I can see his cock growing harder before he answers. "Mistress, may I please take off Danielle's bra. Pretty please?"

When he calls me Mistress, my brain buzzes again and a surge of power runs straight to my pussy and I somehow become even more wet. Oh, fuck, this is awesome.

"Yes, but remove it nice and slow so I can enjoy the view, and then I want you to suck on her nipples, each one for a minute."

Danielle grins at me in approval, and then closes her eyes as Jon removes her lingerie and takes a nipple in his mouth. Her soft moan reaches me, and I run my hand between my legs and slip my finger under my panties and between my wet folds. While Jon licks and sucks, and she moans, I lean back in the chair and rub my clit. I keep my eyes open, watching them, and Danielle's growing passion excites me further.

"Danielle, I want you to remove your panties and spread your legs so Jon can see what he's getting for his birthday."

"Yes, Mistress."

Her response is another zing to my brain. I can't believe I just ordered some woman to open her legs for my husband, but the thrill that runs through me when she takes her panties off, tosses them across the room, and lies on her back and spreads herself wide open is amazing.

I stand up and walk to the end of the bed so I can admire the full view of her pussy. I'm about to tell Jon to climb between her legs and start licking, but change my mind. Why should he get all the fun?

"Jon, I want you to stay there, stroking yourself nice and slow, while you watch me with Danielle."

Not giving him time to answer, I climb onto the bed and settle in between her legs. Starting at her knees, I kiss my way up her inner thigh. When I reach her pussy, I glance over at Jon to double check he's following orders. Like a good boy, he's doing exactly what I asked. His hard cock is in his hand, and he's sliding over the tip and down the base slowly while staring intently at Danielle's spread legs. This is probably the first actual pussy he's seen in years that wasn't mine or a porn star's, so I don't begrudge his fascination with her. He better get his fill tonight, though, because it's not every day you find someone this hot and willing to fuck strangers.

Using both hands, I push back her folds, exposing her soft wetness and clit. I lean in and flick my tongue across the sensitive bud, and Danielle gasps and moans. The adorable high-pitched gasp gets me, and I want to hear more of it. I dive in and feast, sucking and licking with a gentle but firm tongue. Since I've never been with another woman before, I didn't really know what to expect, but the taste of her is pleasant. She's slightly sweet, mixed with something else undefinable that I assume is her own special essence.

She moans louder as I lick faster. Her soft, musky scent makes me dizzy and when a gush of wetness hits my tongue, my need to be in control ramps up. I've always considered men easy to please and figured a woman would be harder, and knowing that Danielle is loving what I'm doing is a complete power trip. I need to make her come, and I want Jon to watch me do it.

Ignoring Jon, I focus all my attention on Danielle. I slide two fingers into her pussy, and she groans when I slowly finger fuck her while continuing to suck on her clit. Danielle's breathing picks up, and she arches against my mouth. I sense she's getting close to her orgasm. I pick up speed and I'm rewarded with sharper moans as she grinds against my face.

Spearing my fingers inside her roughly, she gasps out, "Oh, my god," repeatedly, and I can't help but smile against her pussy. It's fucking hot to hear another woman say that and know I'm the one controlling her pleasure.

With each press of my fingers inside her, wetness gushes out and when she bucks underneath me and groans loudly, I can feel her entire body quiver with her orgasm. I continue to lick her, but more gently as she comes down from her peak, and only when she relaxes fully do I move away.

I sit up on my knees. Jon has a pained, tortured expression on his face, but he's still stroking himself slowly. Oh, what a good boy. I hold the two fingers that I just removed from Danielle's pussy out towards him.

"Suck my fingers clean," I command, and he groans and leans over to fasten his lips on the offered digits.

Well, shit. If I had known how amazing a threesome was going to be, I would have advocated for one years ago. When he's done cleaning up my sticky fingers, I climb off the bed and sit back in the chair. Danielle's orgasm relaxed her, but Jon appears worked up. They both look at me expectantly.

Deciding to not make this too easy on him, I question, "Jon, do you want to fuck Danielle?"

"Yes, Mistress. Please?"

The tingle in my brain urges me to make him beg.

"I want you to beg me to allow you to fuck her."

Jon groans and stops rubbing himself, as if he can't stroke and think at the same time. I smile inwardly.

"I didn't say you could stop touching yourself. Keep stroking and beg."

Jon moans loudly at my order, but starts rubbing himself again. He's quiet for a few moments, and I can tell he's trying to think.

"Mistress, may I please, please, please fuck Danielle? I'm desperate to come and it's my birthday."

I'm tempted to tell him his begging sucks, but this was his first try at it, and it is his birthday.

I glance over at Danielle and want to make sure we have her consent still. "Danielle, do you want him to fuck you?"

Her voice is soft when she answers. "Yes, Mistress."

Each time they address me as "Mistress", the buzz in my brain increases. I need Jon to destroy Danielle's pussy.

"Okay, then. I'm going to sit here playing with myself. Danielle, get up on all fours at the end of the bed. Jon, stand behind her. I want you to fuck her harder than you've ever fucked before. If I'm not pleased, I will stop you both and then you'll have to watch me get off without touching yourselves. Understand?"

They both quickly nod and say, "Yes, Mistress," in unison, which gives me that pleasant zing.

"Well, get to it," I order, and neither of them waste time getting into position.

I lean back in the chair again and bring my fingers to my sopping hole while Jonathan seizes Danielle by the hips and thrusts into her. Both of them groan, and Jon doesn't slow down. I rub faster while Jon fucks her harder, and I have to admit he's bringing his A game. He's never fucked me this violently, and I think it's time I demand he be more rough with me. He obviously can, if motivated.

Watching Jon fuck someone else is so completely erotic, and the pleasure increases as I finger myself and furiously rub my clit. Danielle moans louder and knowing she's getting close to another orgasm is edging me closer to mine. When Danielle cries out in ecstasy and bucks against Jon, seeing her lose herself to pleasure pushes me over the abyss and I give a loud, "Oh, my god," as I come hard with my fingers deep in my pussy. I hear Jon growl loudly as he comes, and I finally close my eyes as the waves of delight rush over my body.

The orgasm subsides and I'm lost in my own world for a minute while my body relaxes and the rush of power drains from my brain, leaving me exhausted. When I open my eyes, Danielle and Jon are both lying on the bed. Danielle is curled up behind him, tucked against him with her arms around his waist as the big spoon. It's adorable, and I crawl onto the bed with them and snuggle in front of Jon as his little spoon. Settling in, I give an enormous yawn as he pulls me closer to him, kisses my ear, and whispers.

"Thank you, Kitten, for the wonderful present."

I smile sleepily, content to be Kitten again despite how much fun I had directing Danielle and Jon. Maybe we need to do this next year for his birthday too?

The End

# CHLOE'S HOTWIFE BIRTHDAY

.

# CHAPTER 1

I'm startled awake from a light doze on the couch when my husband, Jon, drops a thick paperback book in my lap. I'd fallen asleep while waiting for him to get home from work. I'm about to chew him out for scaring me, but I focus on the book instead. It's a bodice-ripping romance novel with a gorgeous nobleman on the cover and a fair maiden acting all demure, as if she doesn't want Mr. Hunky all over her.

"Uh, what's this?"

Not wanting to be rude, I don't tell him this is not my preferred genre. I'm more of a contemporary romantic humor type of gal. I like a good laugh while the main character does stupid shit I'd probably do while she's attempting to find love. Think *Bridget Jones's Diary*. But shouldn't Jon know this by now?

"Well, hello to you too, Miranda."

Jon grins at my lack of greeting, sits down on the couch, and pats his lap. That's his signal he wants to snuggle, and today I decide to stretch out with my head in on his legs. I gaze up at him, raise my eyebrows, and wait for his answer.

"You remember my friend Ethan from college?"

I try to temper my expression because, of course, I remember his damn friend, Ethan. Every single time he mentions a friend's name, he prefaces with it something stupid like "Do you remember that guy...." I know it's just his style of speech, but sometimes he acts as if I'm an idiot who remembers nothing.

He doesn't meet up with Ethan often. They have lunch or get together every couple of months, so it's not as if they're best pals or anything. But Jon has a fun time with him and has stayed in contact all these years. I've even met Ethan a few times.

Instead of blurting out what I'm really thinking, I simply say, "Yes, I remember Ethan."

"I met him for lunch today. His wife wrote that book, and he gave me a signed copy to give to you."

*Oh, huh?* I look at the book with more interest and flip the cover over to check out the back. The author's picture reveals a very attractive woman in her mid-20s with ash blonde hair. *Way to go, Ethan.* Ethan is cute, but in a nerdy way. I wouldn't have expected him to score someone like this, and a successful writer at that. I mean, I assume once you're published, people consider you a success... right? The cover is shiny and professional. Chloe must do pretty well for herself.

I fan through the pages and notice Chloe wrote, "For Miranda," and signed her name, so this was a pre-planned gift. Well, that was sweet of her. I finally realize Jon's been watching me intently this entire time while I check out the book.

"What?" I'm defensive, as if I'm doing something wrong.

"Uh, so Ethan was telling me Chloe's birthday is coming up in a couple of weeks...."

My stomach drops. Oh fuck, he wants me to go to a damn surprise party with him. He knows I hate big gatherings and surprise parties are the worst because you have to get there 30 minutes early and stand around in the dark and watch the person pretend to be surprised when the lights flip on. This is not how I intend to spend my evening, especially when I don't know anyone else — personally autographed book or not.

"And I may have told him before about our hotwife agreement...."

*Wait, what's this*? I'm more alert and focus on Jon. I'm dubious about where this is going, but he now has my attention. Jon rushes out the last part quickly with a whoosh of breath, as if he's nervous.

"And Ethan mentioned how Chloe has a lesbian fantasy and he wants to see if you'd be willing to be a surprise gift to her."

I blink up at Jon, uncertain what to say. ANOTHER birthday gift? Jesus Christ, how many times am I going to do birthdays? This will be the... third time — no, fourth if you count Jon's. Wait, maybe three? I mentally calculate in my head—Harold, Alec, Jon—right, this would be the fourth birthday.

I'm about ready to tell him to shove it and that I'm done with being a gift, but I glance back at Chloe's picture on the book. She really *is* gorgeous. My pussy throbs, and I'm reminded of my threesome with Jon and Danielle for Jon's recent birthday. Going down on Danielle was fabulous. *Uh, wait....*

"This wouldn't include Ethan, would it?"

Jon laughs at me. "No, this would be just you and Chloe. He didn't even ask to watch on Zoom."

Jon enjoys teasing me about the time he watched me get railed by all my bosses over video, and keeps saying I should offer video to the spouses for these celebrations. But I'm not doing any more birthdays, right? The weight of the book is heavy in my hand, and my palm tingles where it connects with the cover. A gush of wetness hits my panties, and I briefly consider several hours alone with Chloe. Uh... guess my slutty pussy wants this.

Not wanting to look like I'm making a big deal out of it, I shrug at Jon. "Sure, I'll do it."

Jon caresses my cheek. "Thank you, Kitten. Ethan's going to be thrilled, and I want all the details when you get home."

Jon's hardening cock under my head supports his words. Oh, yeah, my sweet, goofy husband is all into the idea of me explaining exactly what Chloe and I do together. I stand up and hold out my hand to him.

"Come with me to the bedroom, and I'll tell you my ideas."

Jon didn't need telling twice. He's up in a flash, bats my offered hand away, and chases me into the bedroom.

# CHAPTER 2

Ethan decided he didn't want me to surprise Chloe and expect her to open her legs to another woman with zero notice, so he told her in advance about the gift to make sure she was all on board. I guess the pictures of me from our recent beach vacation that Jon emailed over helped convince her that I would be an ideal first-time lesbian experience. After that, she and I took over the plans and left the men out. We agreed to meet for coffee a week before her birthday to avoid any unnecessary awkwardness the night we hook up.

I didn't get enough sleep the night before our coffee date because I stayed up late reading her book, hoping to get some insider tips on the way her mind works from the way she writes. The book was better than I expected, but it made me even more anxious to meet her.

I wake up with butterflies in my stomach in the morning, and as I get ready to head out for coffee, the fluttering in my belly intensifies. I hem and haw over what to wear and end up on the chair in my closet giggling at myself. God, you'd think I was getting ready for a first date.

Meeting a woman I'm going to sleep with differs from seeing a guy for the first time. Guys seem to be way less picky about who they shove their dicks into, but I want Chloe to think I'm sexy. My cute awkwardness might not translate well for women when they're looking for a potential sexual partner. I pause and consider how hurt I'd be if I got home and there was a message from Chloe saying she changed her mind. I shake my head to clear the thought. Focus, Miranda... must find clothes.

I select my sexiest pair of skinny jeans, and a sheer, black, long-sleeved blouse I can pair with a lace camisole. For shoes, I go with some comfortable wedge sandals that show off my purple pedicure. I even pick out my jewelry with care, and choose some delicate silver dangling earrings with a matching pendant. Checking myself out in the mirror, I'm satisfied that I look casual, yet hot. I'd do me, if I was the one choosing.

Chloe is waiting at an outside table when I get to the coffee shop. She looks different from, but enough like, her author picture that I recognize her. She doesn't notice me at first, and I check her out as I'm walking up. Chloe's wearing a short yellow, floral sundress and strappy high-heeled sandals. Her crossed legs are sexy and my fingers twitch. I want to run my hands up the inside of her legs and imagine kissing her knee. Chloe's cleavage impresses in the dress and I wonder for a split second what type of bra she has on under the dress that creates such lovely pillows above the neckline. I wish I'd worn a more revealing shirt to showcase my own assets since my breasts are perky, full, and have nice up-tilt nipples. My outfit is tame compared to her lush sexuality. I don't know where this newfound appreciation of women came from, but I desperately need to touch Chloe all over and make her moan.

I shake my head to clear the sexual daze and plant myself in the chair across from her. Plopping down as if I'm meeting any casual acquaintance, I realize my mistake. *Ugh, blah.* I mentally cringe at how ungraceful I am.

Chloe doesn't care, and beams a greeting at me. "Hi, Miranda!"

Her voice is sensuous, and I wasn't expecting my pussy to pulsate from hearing her speak, nor the sudden flush of warmth spreading from my groin outward. I set my purse down on the table, but the immediate sexual attraction turns my brain to mush and my arm knocks my purse off onto the ground.

Blurting out, "Shit!" I make a wild dash to catch it.

I'm unable to grab it, the top tips upside down, while the contents splat out in one enormous pile. It's not just my loins that are warm and flushed now. I can feel my cheeks burning as well. We both lean over to fish the various items out from under the table.

I babble about how uncoordinated I am, as Chloe deposits various items on the glass-topped table. She pauses with a bottle of purple nail polish.

"Is this the color on your toes?"

Hah, guess she got a look at my feet while she was under there.

"Yep." I glance at the bottle she's holding while stuffing everything else in my purse.

Chloe flips the bottle over and reads the name out loud. "The Sound of Vibrance. I like it." She hands the nail polish to me and I slip it in with the rest of the jumble. On a good day, my purse is a mess, but now it's on a whole other level. This is going to take some time to organize again.

Once I'm certain we missed nothing on the ground, I lean back in the metal patio chair and puff out my breath.

"Sorry, I'm such a klutz."

Chloe grins. "Don't worry, we've all been there."

I notice she doesn't have a drink yet and ask, "Want me to go in and order us something?"

Her silvery laugh rings out before her answer. "Why don't I do it? I know the guy at the counter and he usually gives me free drinks."

Not one to turn down free anything, I request an iced chai tea with heavy cream. She leaves her purse at the table, and I tip my head in confusion as she strolls into the coffee shop with a sensual swagger. That's brave of her to assume she will get it for free. I'd die of embarrassment if I tried that and then had to come back out for my purse.

The front wall of the cafe has tall windows, so I can see everything inside the store. My eyes widen in surprise when she leans over the counter with the fingertips of one hand caressing her lips, and the other hand lightly running up the cashier guy's arm. The young guy fumbles with the register and rings something in. When it spits out the receipt, he tosses it in the trash. Chloe gives his forearm a last squeeze and turns to look out the window at me. I swear she winks at me, but I can't be sure from this distance.

A few minutes later, she saunters to the table with our drink order, and I stare at her in amazement. She's the type of woman that women like me dream about and wish we could be. How did Ethan catch such an adorable creature? And this girl is down to fuck me? No way in hell I won't see a "thanks but no thanks" email when I get home, and now that I'm assuming there is no point in trying, the tension in my upper back and neck ease. At least I'm getting some nice eye candy and a free drink out of this — plus my autographed book.

Now that I'm relaxed, we joke and giggle like old friends as we share war stories about our marriages. As she tells me about Ethan, I can see why he and Jon stayed in contact. They both are a couple of lovable dorks. I sense Chloe has a bit of a bite to her sense of humor, but I appreciate a little sass.

Since we hadn't talked about the upcoming birthday, I'm surprised when Chloe brings it up. "Miranda, why do you want to sleep with me?"

I almost choke on the last of my tea. *Oooh, okay. Guess it's a fair question.*

My heart is pounding and I'm unsure how to word that I'm a hotwife. "Well... did Ethan tell you anything about my... uh... lifestyle?"

Chloe nods, so I continue. "I sort of have a thing for birthdays lately. I keep agreeing to be someone else's gift."

She says nothing, but takes a sip of her drink. When she sets the cup down, there is a drop of moisture on her lips. When her tongue darts out to lick it off, a flush steals over me. My cooch kicks into high gear, and the urge to bear down against the metal chair and wiggle around hits me. I force myself to sit still. Shit, she's hot.

Chloe is hesitant when she asks the next question. "Do YOU want to sleep with a woman?"

Instead of answering, I sweep my eyes down the length of her body and back up. Her entire body is visible through the glass tabletop. I stare deeply into her eyes and Chloe blushes. A tiny bead of per-spiration runs down the column of her neck and the desire to lick it overwhelms me. It's a warm day, so I bet she'd be salty and sweet. When I focus on her neck, I can see her pulse throbbing.

When she shifts in her chair and opens her legs slightly, I'm lost. Pleasure aches flood my body and my heartbeat and stomach flutter. *Oh god, I think I want her more than I wanted Danielle.*

I stand up, and Chloe squeaks in surprise while watching me, confused.

"I need to use the restroom. Come with me?" I quirk an eyebrow at her, daring her.

She doesn't hesitate and grabs her purse and cup, and we both toss the drinks in the garbage on the way into the cafe. The bathrooms are small, one-person rooms with locking doors. As soon as we're in the room, I shove the door closed and flip the lock over so that the "in use" indicator shows red. *Oh yeah, this bathroom is about to be used.*

Chloe is standing in the middle of the room facing me. I turn towards her and press my back against the door for a moment before using my arms to push off and stalk her for the three steps it takes to reach her. I nudge her in the direction of the wall behind her, and when it stops our momentum, I capture her lips in a passionate kiss.

One hand is on her cheek, and I'm amazed at how tiny and delicate she is. I know I won't break her, but equal parts of my brain war against each other. Half of me wants to ravish her, and the other half wants to protect her. When she sighs against my lips, I decide—ravishment it is.

I press against her harder and dart my tongue into her mouth. She tastes like mint and coffee, and my body aches for more. My panties are damp and my nipples stiffen while I break off the kiss and nibble down her neck. She arches her back and moans when I cup her breasts in my hands and rub my thumbs across her hard pebbles underneath the thin fabric of her sundress and bra.

I momentarily wonder how I'm going to fuck her in this bathroom, but realize that unless I'm going to set her on the sink or we're getting down on the floor, there aren't any options. Guess I'll have to improvise. I really want to taste her pussy, but I'll save that for her birthday, if given the chance.

While I bite and suck on her neck, I move my hands down to her hips and slide up her dress. I hook my fingers into the top band of her panties and push them down. She shimmies her hips a little, and her knickers fall to the floor, and she steps one foot out so her legs can spread.

I murmur, "Good girl," against her collar and a jolt of lust hits me. *Oh, yeah, this feeling again.* I haven't felt this way since the threesome. An intense high washes over me. Suddenly, instead of tasting her, I have the urge to force Chloe to her knees and make her lick my pussy, but I'm the one in skinny jeans and she's the one whose panties are on the floor. I push the neediness away and focus on what I'm going to do to Chloe.

Slipping my hand between her legs, I find that her thighs are damp from her soaked pussy. My fingers part her delicate folds and seek her clit while she mewls out adorable gasps. I tease her bud in soft circles as she grinds against my hand, forcing me to rub harder. *Oooh, guess someone likes it a little rough*. I bring three fingers together and switch to a brisk stroke. Chloe's loud moans echo against the tiles.

Knowing it's possible the tables close to the bathroom can hear us gives me a naughty thrill, and I hope Chloe is a screamer. My free hand pulls down the top of her sundress, exposing a beige lace balconette bra, and I kiss her cleavage and hum in delight. I've never worn this type of bra before, but it explains why the dress looks amazing on her. Pulling the straps down, I'm able to push her fleshy globes out of the cups. Her dusty-pink nipples are a little larger than mine, and I latch my mouth onto the nipple and continue the onslaught of her clit while I suck.

Chloe's gasps and moans drive me crazy and my panties are a wet mess. I'm determined to make her come so I can go home and pounce on Jon. I want to ride him while I tell him how fucking hot Chloe is and how I made her lose her mind in the cafe bathroom. Even if she declines me after this, she'll have her lesbian experience to fantasize about.

As I suck and pull on Chloe's nipples with my mouth, I ease up on her clit for a moment to finger fuck her. She gasps as I press two fingers in and she rotates her hips in rhythm with the thrust of my hand. I alternate between furiously rubbing her clit and pressing into her pussy, and her cries and moans increase. *Oh yeah, she might be a screamer.* The surge of power in my head increases to where I am wholly focused on her pleasure.

When her legs tense and her back bows, I know she's about to come. I concentrate on her nipple in my mouth and her clit under my fingers until her entire body spasms and she clamps a hand over her mouth to stifle her moans. She jerks against me and I ease up on the rubbing until I'm back to doing soft circles as she floats down from her peak. Dang it, she didn't scream so I hope there is a next time. I still have the urge to make her lose control.

I kiss her softly as I remove my hand from between her legs. "Did you like that?"

"Mmmhmmm..." Chloe is incapable of a complete sentence, and she's leaning against the wall for support.

I put my back to the wall next to her and wrap my arm around her shoulder, letting her slump against me for more support. After a minute, I can tell she's coming around as she straightens up and looks at me.

Chloe's eyes sparkle and she grins. "Best trip to the cafe I've ever had."

I laugh with her and wash my hands at the sink. I can see her in the mirror and I admire her legs and breasts as she pulls up her panties and adjusts the bra back in place. When she's decent, we both exit the restroom.

There is only one table occupied that I would guess was within hearing distance. A couple is at the table closest to the restroom and has a baby in a stroller with them. They both stare at us as we come out. The guy, whom I assume is the husband, has a hungry look in his eye. The woman tries to hide a smirk when we walk past.

Chloe and I part ways outside the cafe. She gives my hand a little squeeze as a goodbye, thanks me for a lovely time, and promises to message me. I stand and watch her walk away for a moment and sigh.

Damn it, why did I fulfill her fantasy before her birthday? Now I'm never going to get to taste her sweet pussy.

Realizing Jon is waiting at home for me, I pull out my phone and text him a peach and a water squirting emoji. He instantly messages back with, "WHAT?!!!!" I giggle out loud and text that I'll give him all the details when I get home, but I expect him naked in bed when I get there. His reply of, "Yes, Mistress," jolts me. *Holy fuck, am I a Domme?*

# CHAPTER 3

My head is still spinning when I wake up the next morning from my wild night with Jon, and the first thing I notice is a text from Chloe.

`Do you have a strap-on?`

Wait, what's this? Sitting up in bed, I'm now fully alert. I mean, I don't have a strap-on... yet. I'm not 100 percent sure where this conversation is heading, but I like the direction and decide to lie.

`Yes, I do. Why?`

I'm breathless, and my slutty pussy springs to life. She got plenty of action yesterday as I rode Jon hard and made him beg to come, but guess she's still interested in more.

`Bring it on Saturday.`

Fuck yeah! She still wants to celebrate her birthday. My hands tremble as I reply.

`Sounds like a fun time.`

I include a smiley face and she replies with a thumbs up and a fire emoji. There is a lightness in my chest and I hug myself. I'm giggling with excitement when Jon walks into the bedroom carrying two coffee mugs. He pauses and grins at my happiness.

"What's got you all giggly this morning?"

Instead of answering, I blurt out, "Want to go to the sex toy shop with me today?"

He laughs out loud at the question as he sets a mug on my night-stand. "What do we need there?"

"I want to buy a strap-on."

Jon goes to take a sip of his coffee but pauses with the mug right at his lips. His eyes widen.

"Uh, Kitten... don't you think we should talk about this first? Maybe you could try a finger and we work up to bigger stuff?"

His answer makes me giggle harder, and I struggle to talk.

"It's... for... Chloe!"

"Oh, well, that's fine then." He kisses my forehead and wanders out of the bedroom with his coffee.

The laughter subsides, and I take a sip of my coffee. Hey! He never answered me about going to the sex toy shop. I'm about to climb out of bed and hunt him down when I realize an even bigger question. HE WANTS ME TO DO BUTT STUFF? My head spins as I imagine pegging Jon with my new strap-on. *Oh, yeah, it's happening.* I stalk out of the room to find him. He's coming with me to choose this strap-on now.

# CHAPTER 4

Clutching a tote with my new purchase inside, I head out the door on Saturday to meet up with Chloe. I'd also tossed some lube in the tote in case she asks for anal, as well as a sparkly plastic tiara so I can crown her the birthday girl. I check my phone one last time to make sure I remembered the driving directions. She'd made Ethan spring for a hotel room because she didn't want either of our husbands interrupting us. Jon's going out to drink with some friends tonight anyway, so I doubt he would have, but I like the idea of making her come all over clean hotel sheets.

The room she booked was at a swanky hotel, which I wasn't expecting. I'm in a carefree, silly mood and, as a joke, I'm wearing a long trench coat and black thigh-high boots, with only a black three-piece garter set underneath. I put my hair in a high ponytail so when I eat her out, it won't get in the way, and to complete the look, I went with bright red lipstick and large silver hoop earrings. Chloe texted me the room number and told me to come up, so as I strut across the lobby with only my handbag, I'm positive I look like an exotic dancer heading upstairs for a party.

An elderly couple in the elevator with me almost gives me a *Pretty Woman* movie vibe because the older guy keeps staring at me. I want to be like Kit in the movie and say, "fifty bucks, Grandpa. For seventy-five the wife can watch." I just wink at him when the wife doesn't notice, and giggle after they get out a few floors before me. Hope Chloe is ready for playful Miranda.

When Chloe opens the door to the hotel room, she runs her arm up the open door frame and poses for me while I stand in awe. She's wearing a purple lace lingerie set, and my mouth actually starts watering at the glimpse of her amazing breasts and nipples through the sheer fabric. My heart pounds and I feel myself growing wet. My hands ache to touch her, and I can't help myself, so I lean in and give her a passionate kiss and cup one of her breasts, gently squeezing it.

She moans into my mouth and just that little noise triggers something in me. I push her into the room, close the door, and drop my tote on the floor. She moves to sit on the bed to watch me as I remove my boots. When I unbelt my trench coat and toss it over a chair, Chloe, delighted, grins at me at whistles at my garter belt and stockings.

"I can't believe you only wore that under your coat!" She's laughing, but has a hungry look in her eyes.

When I spot the smears of my red lipstick around her mouth, a shiver runs through me. I want to muss her up and wipe the grin off her face and replace it with rapture. Her ash-blonde hair is loose and I realize that won't work for my plans. I pick up my bag, set it on the dresser, and dig through it. I think I saw a hair tie in there, and when I find it, I brandish it towards her triumphantly. She's puzzled, so I walk over to her and stand close enough to cup her chin with my hand, forcing her to look up at me.

"I'm going to go into the bathroom to wash my lipstick off. When I get back, I want your hair in a low ponytail." I press the hair tie into her palm and she doesn't answer.

In the bathroom, I examine myself in the mirror. I'm flushed, and my nipples are hard and visible through my bra. My hands shake a little as I use a tissue to wipe my mouth. The red lipstick was probably a bad idea, but I needed the confidence boost. I remove the silver hoop earrings and leave them on the counter. I don't need her thighs ripping them out of my ears as I eat her pussy.

Back in the bedroom, Chloe's hair is in a neat ponytail and she's sitting demurely on the edge of the bed still, as if she's waiting for my instruction. *Oh fuck, that's hot.* I want to push her back and sample her while she moans, but I need to know something first.

"Chloe, what do you want out of tonight?"

She obviously wants to be fucked with a strap-on, but I'm curious what else she's expecting. Chloe hesitates before replying, but when she does, her voice is clear and sensual.

"I want the full lesbian experience."

*Hmmm, that could mean a lot of things.* "What exactly do you mean, Chloe?"

Chloe looks down and traces the flowers on the comforter. She doesn't meet my eyes and haltingly admits, "I want to go down on you."

*Oh, well now.* For a moment I'm back in the bathroom with her at the cafe and have the urge to force her to her knees again, and this time I'm going to follow through. Putting my foot up on the chair, I unclasp my garters and make sure she's tracking me as I roll my stockings down and pull them off. I leave the garter belt on, and I'm still wearing my panties and bra when I approach Chloe. Her chest is noticeably heaving, so I know I'm having an effect on her.

Pausing in front of her, I study her. When she darts her eyes away and can't meet my gaze, the buzz in my brain dies down and I have a moment of clarity. I could get Chloe to do whatever the fuck I wanted, and she would thank me for it. My entire body tingles with that thought, and the brain buzz whooshes back with a vengeance. The rush overwhelms me, and my voice is harsh.

"Chloe, get on your knees. NOW."

Her eyes widen, but she dutifully slides off the bed onto her knees directly in front of me, with her gaze towards the floor. There isn't much space between us, so she's almost touching me. Chloe didn't strike me as a passive woman based on the stories I've heard about her sexual exploits from Jon — who presumably heard them from Ethan — but she's acting submissive to me. She's the type of woman who knows how to get what she wants, and it's possible, based on our experience at the cafe, that she perceived this is the way to handle me. If so, she's right and I want to fuck her so hard her head spins and she doesn't know her own name.

"Chloe."

When I say her name, she glances up at me.

"You are going to be good for Mistress and take off her panties."

Calling myself Mistress makes me feel in control, so I roll with it.

"And then you are going to lick up the inside of my thighs. Take your time with it. I want you to savor the experience. And then I want you to slide your mouth over my pussy and make me come. If you can lick as good as you can obey, I will give you a treat and use the strap-on. Do you understand?"

Chloe nods and answers, "Yes."

There's a mirror on the wall across the room and I want to watch, so I move closer to the bed, stopping when I'm standing with the mirror directly across from me. Chloe half crawls, half pivots to follow me. Looking in the mirror, I see myself gazing back, all sexy in my black lingerie set, with the back of Chloe's head and shoulder in view. The mirror just barely shows her bra strap, which I can't wait to undo.

I fight the urge to force her to call me Mistress. Since she just met me, I'll cut her some slack. Plus, we didn't exactly talk about what would happen if I got all dominant on her, which in hindsight we should have, since I had an inkling it would go this direction. Vowing to not become a strict Domme on her, I keep quiet and stand still while she runs her hands up the outside of my thighs, hooks her fingers into the top band of my panties and slides them down. I step out of them and spread my legs, giving her room to continue with her instructions.

Chloe starts at my knee, kissing and licking her way towards my pussy. I look in the mirror and it's almost as if I'm watching a porno. *When did my life become this*? I have a desirable woman on the floor in front of me who's about to eat me out. I shiver, but I'm not sure if it's because of my thoughts or if it's Chloe's moist kisses. As she's using her mouth on my thighs, her hands continue to caress the outside of my legs. Her touch is soft — much softer than Jon's—and twice she hits an extra sensitive area and I want to giggle because it's ticklish.

The closer she gets to my pussy, the wetter I become. To give her more room, I put my right foot up on the bed, spreading myself open for her. I'm glad I trimmed the kitty for this weekend since Chloe is getting a full-on view of my pussy. The Miranda in the mirror looks super slutty, and I love it. Chloe takes the invitation and leans in to kiss and lick me. She's tentative at first, but when her soft tongue touches my clit for the first time, I moan and close my eyes. *God, this is amazing*.

My reaction spurs her on, and she licks and sucks with gusto. I was unprepared for how erotic it would be to have Chloe between my legs. I crack my eyes open so I can watch the show. The Miranda in the mirror is full of lust, and I'm aching and needy as Chloe continues to lick my bud. Every brush of her tongue sends spirals of pleasure through my body, but I want more.

I demand, "Chloe, slide a finger inside of me."

She replies, but it's muffled by my cooch. When she obeys me and brings a hand up to join her mouth, I get an intense rush of power. She finger fucks me while continuing to lick, and my thighs tense and I moan as waves of bliss wash over me. I'm going to come soon and I press Chloe's face hard into my pussy, leaving my hands on her head to force her to stay there. She intensifies the licking and I moan out long and hard as I peak. I'm shaking and trembling as the pleasure radiates from my core. My pussy spasms against her fingers and she slows down the pace of her tongue and fingers, tasting my juices and bringing me down gently.

I push her head back gently and bring my leg down off the bed. She was great, and I came fast. I pet her hair.

"Good girl."

She bounces on her knees a little, and I smile at her face, shiny with my juices. I consider getting her a towel, but I'm going to make her use the sheets instead. Pulling the comforter off the bed, I pat the edge.

"Get up onto the bed. I want to taste you."

Chloe lets out a soft moan as she replies, "Yes, please."

She sits on the edge, and I push her shoulders down so she's lying with her legs dangling off the side. I get on my knees in front of the bed, slide my arms under her thighs and pull her towards me. She widens her legs, exposing her pussy fully and I feast my eyes on the delicate pink folds. She's swollen and dripping wet. *Someone enjoyed licking me.*

Leaning forward, I spread her pussy lips with my thumbs and slowly tongue her entire crease. She moans and thrashes, and when she jerks her hips, I let up on the pressure a little since she seems extra sensitive. She relaxes as I lick softly. Her moans and little gasps ping my brain and it takes all my control to not get rough. My head spins from the taste and smell of her, and I'm getting turned on again from the adorable sounds she's making.

When she groans, "Oh, fuck," and her hips buck under my mouth, I move my mouth away before she comes.

Chloe cries out, "Why?" in a sad mewl and I have to hold in my grin. I've been on the receiving end of almost coming when Jon goes down on me, and now I understand why he stops. Leaving her needy and desperate for my fake cock is a power trip.

"I'll be right back with your treat."

Chloe sighs out a pathetic, "Okay," and this time I really do smile as I head into the bathroom with the strap-on box. I dump the contents on the counter and realize I should have practiced before now. Since I lied and said I had one, she's expecting me to know how to use it. I peek out into the bedroom and she's still lying on the bed and hasn't moved. I click the bathroom door closed and get down to business with the strap-on.

Close to ten minutes later, after practicing thrusting and rolling my hips, I strut out, proud of my six-inch cock. I stop and glance in the full-length mirror and wiggle my hips to make it sway. The harness is on firmly, but the dildo still has a bit of maneuverability. I suppose real cocks do as well, so this is realistic-ish.

Chloe, propped up on her elbows, watches me from the bed. As I approach the bed, she scoots to the edge and sits up.

"Miranda, can I touch your breasts?"

Her request gives me pause. I'm feeling the vibe from my mighty cock and plan to fuck her, but she wants the full lesbian experience and I don't want to send her home wondering what it feels like to suck another girl's tits. I unhook my bra and drop it on the floor.

"Yes, you may."

I stand close to her, and when the dildo wags in front of her face, she giggles.

"Why don't I lie down so you can reach me easier?"

I crawl onto the bed and roll onto my back. The dildo sticking straight up makes me laugh and Chloe giggles some more. She can play around all she wants now, but I plan on having her moaning soon. My brain turns off when she snuggles next to me and runs her hand over my breast and tweaks the nipple.

Her slow and cautious exploration turns me on, and when she bends over to suck on my nipple, I moan. *Oh, fuck.* I already got my pleasure, and I wanted this to be about her now, but I can't help thinking of all the ways I could make her serve me again.

She gets rougher with my breasts and pinches the nipples harder, so I decide to end her fun. I push her off me gently and sit up.

I'm breathless, but still able to sound commanding. "Get on your hands and knees in the middle of the bed."

She quickly complies, and I get on my knees behind her. It's surreal to be on this end of things with a woman presenting her ass and pussy to me, but I love it. I slide my hand against her wet folds and massage her clit. She's still soaking wet, and she gasps as I rub her swollen bean in circles.

I want to make sure she comes from the dildo, so I pull my hand back and hold on to her hips with one hand while I guide the dildo into her pussy with the other. Seeing it disappear inch by inch into her hole is arousing, and she's moaning as I push the toy all the way inside of her and pause.

"Does this feel good?"

Chloe moans louder. "Yesss...."

I pull out and experiment with a hard thrust. When she groans, I take it to mean she likes it a little rough. *Oh, I can do that.* Not trusting that I will keep the dildo poking into the right spot without holding onto it, I grasp the base with one hand and pound into her pussy a few times. Chloe squeals and presses back to meet my thrusts. I pull out fully and sit back on my knees to appreciate the view of her drenched cunt. She wiggles her hips and glances over her shoulder at me.

"Why'd you stop?"

I smile mischievously. "So I can do this."

I smack her right ass cheek as hard as I can with my open palm. She groans, and I quickly smack the left side as well. I continue to spank her, alternating sides, and I get into a smooth rhythm after a couple of whacks. Chloe groans between each one, but doesn't protest. I'm breathing harshly and all turned on. Wishing I could continue, I know I need to be in control and force myself to stop. I'd guess I gave her ten sharp spanks per cheek and her ass has a nice soft pink glow. I immediately thrust the toy back into her quivering pussy.

Chloe groans out, "Oh, fuck," and lowers her head to the bed so she's at an angle as I drill into her. Testing out if she likes it when I grind instead of thrusting, she whimpers and rolls her hips. *Jesus, this is unbelievably hot.* I should have fucked women years ago. I didn't realize that being on this end of a strap-on and observing a woman in the throes of ecstasy would exhilarate me.

When Chloe pants out, "Fuck me," repeatedly, I know she's getting close. Still gripping the base of the dildo, I switch back to hard thrusts and hold onto her hip with the other hand so I can pull her against me. The sound of our skin slapping together when the dildo bottoms out and our harsh breathing fills the room. Chloe better scream at the end of this or I'm going to be unhappy.

To help her along, I demand, "Chloe, rub your clit while I fuck you."

She gasps out a yes and her hand snakes underneath her so she can massage her clit. When her finger finds its home, she groans long and loud.

"Good girl," I huff out between lunges.

Chloe, lost in bliss, is a mindless fucktoy underneath me. I take a hand off her hip and smack her ass sharply, once, before resuming the pounding of her pussy. She jerks underneath me and screams out.

"Oh, my god. I'm coming! I'm coming!"

Her hips grind tiny circles against me and she trembles beneath my hand. Her moaning peaks and then subsides, so I slow down my thrusts. When she relaxes, I pull out fully and crawl up the bed, collapsing on my side facing her. She stays in the same position with her face buried in her arms against the bed for a moment before finally sliding onto her belly, limp.

We're both a sweaty mess. I had no idea how much of a workout wearing the strap-on would be. No wonder why some nights Jon just wants to lie there while I'm on top. This strap-on is a pleasant option, but I bet having a penis with nerve endings is awesome while fucking a woman. The pleasure I got seeing her go crazy, on top of it also bringing me ecstasy—yeah, I wouldn't mind being a guy for a day.

Chloe turns her head towards me and smiles. "Thank you, Miranda. This is a great birthday."

That reminds me of the tiara in my bag.

"I'll be right back. I want to take this off."

I scoot off the end of the bed and fiddle with the harness, unsnapping it and laying it on the dresser. Some of Chloe's juices run down the side onto the wood surface. I'm not leaving that for some poor housekeeper to clean up later, but deciding I'll worry about that when I'm packing to leave, I snag the tiara from the bag, grab two bottles of water from the mini fridge, and climb back up on the bed.

Chloe rolled to her side when I got up. I hand her a bottle of water and slip the tiara on her head while I snuggle in close to her.

"There. Now it's a happy birthday. You're a princess for the night."

She reaches up and fondles the tiara on her head and smiles sleepily. "I've always wanted to be a princess."

I lean over and kiss her nose, knowing this will be a night I'll never forget. I also vow to practice my strap-on skills on my poor husband's unsuspecting ass, so the next time I get the chance to fuck a woman, I'll be better prepared.

After we sip some water, Chloe and I doze for a while. When I wake up before her, I watch her sleep and run my fingers through the end of her ponytail. I giggle quietly when I realize I never did what I planned with her hair. I was going to pull on the tail while I fucked her from behind.

A memory of my boss, Mr. Knight, requesting me to wear pigtails and then forgetting to do anything with them while he fucked me pops into my head. He said he'd use them next time, but he hasn't requested them since. A warmth seeps over me and my pussy springs to life again as I think of Mr. Knight. Maybe I need to wear pigtails to work again soon to tempt him. My birthday is coming up; maybe I'll request a special day with him.

I'm spinning with a scenario involving me and Mr. Knight when Chloe wakes up. She yawns and stretches.

"You're welcome to stay the night, if you want."

I glance around the room. *It is pretty nice.* The idea of fucking Chloe in the shower with the strap-on pops into my head. I lean over and give her a deep kiss. "Yes, I think that's a great idea."

We continue to kiss and then briefly break apart to text our husbands. Jon is probably still out drinking and tipsy by now, so I don't expect a response from him. I briefly type that I'm spending the night and give a bunch of fireworks and squirting water emojis. When I'm done, I set the phone on the nightstand, face down, and focus all my attention on Princess Chloe. This is her night and I want to make it a birthday she'll never forget.

And I did.

The End

# MIRANDA'S HOTWIFE BIRTHDAY

# CHAPTER 1

"Miranda, we need to talk."

Startled, I glance up from the Chloe McBride romance novel I'm devouring. Chloe's husband had given me the book as an enticement to agree to celebrate Chloe's birthday and fulfill a lesbian fantasy of hers. It had been a fabulous night, and having fucked the author makes the story so much better. I'd been curled up all cozy on the couch, lost in the book, but now my husband, Jon, is standing in the kitchen's archway, looking out towards me. My chest tightens and my breathing speeds up. Nothing like your husband saying "We need to talk" to ruin a good reading session.

"Uh, what's up?" I try to hide the anxiety in my voice as I set the book in my lap.

"Work is sending me to Philadelphia for a week."

*Oh, shit. Is that all*? I relax into the cushions. Jon was recently promoted and warned me weeks ago that work was talking about sending him out to their headquarters so he could visit with some bigwigs. I won't mind having the house to myself for a bit, but I don't want him to know the idea of being alone for a few days appeals to me, so I attempt to sound casual.

"Oh yeah, when do you leave?"

Jon doesn't answer immediately, shuffles his feet and studies the floor. I narrow my eyes at him, waiting. This isn't good.

He finally blurts out, "That's the thing, it's over your birthday weekend."

I peep out a small, "Oh."

My birthday is in three weeks and it's on a Saturday this year. I was looking forward to doing something fun with Jon. He told me the world was my oyster and to choose whatever I wanted, and I'd been secretly researching getaways. Twenty-nine isn't anything special, but I've been doing a lot of birthday celebrations for other people lately, and I felt with Jon's new promotion that we deserved a mini holiday. Luckily, my heart isn't set on any destination yet and I was only kicking the idea around.

A stab of disappointment hits me, but I try to make light of it. "That's fine. I didn't know what I wanted to do, anyway. We can celebrate after you get back."

I bite my lip and pick up my book again, ignoring him. It's not his fault work requires him to be gone that weekend, but I can't help wondering why he couldn't ask to go on a different date. I was having fun planning and I know delaying it one or two weeks won't really matter, but what am I going to do on my actual birthday? I don't have any family nearby and my best friend, Dina, is off backpacking across Europe right now and living a fabulous life, so that means a lonely night for me.

Jon comes over to the couch, lies down next to me, and puts his head in my lap. I don't look away from my book, but run my fingers through his hair with the hand not holding the book.

"Miranda."

I focus on him instead of the book and he's looking up at me with his adorable puppy-dog eyes. My heart melts a little. *Shit, why does he have to be so cute?* He makes it hard to stay annoyed with him.

"Kitten, I asked them to change the dates, but that week was the only time that worked for everyone."

Any tension left drains from my body. At least he tried. I close my book and set it on the side table and focus all my attention on Jon, and start combing his hair with both my hands. We're both quiet for a few moments while I braid a tiny clump. He really needs to get a haircut before his trip. It's getting too long and shaggy to be professional when he meets the big bosses in Philadelphia. I'm about to comment about him needing a trim, but Jon breaks my train of thought.

"I was thinking you could have a birthday celebration of your choice while I'm gone."

My hands pause mid-braid. *What is he saying*? The only type of celebrating I've been doing lately involves sex, so that's where my brain immediately goes.

I work on finishing the braid and reply in a neutral tone. "Oh, how so?"

"Well, is there anyone you want to invite over that night?"

A tiny spark of sexual energy zips through me and my pussy wakes up. If I can't spend my birthday with Jon, there's only one other man I'd want to ask, but I doubt Jon's offering what my body thinks he is. A shiver runs through me and my slutty side can't help imagining my boss, Mr. Knight, tying me up and doing wonderfully dirty things to me.

My tone is wistful when I tell Jon, "Dina is still in Europe, and there isn't really anyone else to invite over." I gaze over at the wall and let my mind wander. God, it would be great to have the freedom to just pick up and travel whenever the whim struck me. I have a great life, but sometimes I envy Dina and her solo trips.

"I meant someone for sex."

Another shiver runs down my spine at his words. *Uh... now he's got my attention.*

I look him straight in the eyes and ask, "You'd be okay with that?"

Jon laughs at me. "Oh, Kitten, we had a threesome for my birthday and it was wonderful. I want you to have fun on your day."

My pussy tingles and the temperature of the room seems to rise. *Well, holy hell. Maybe this birthday is salvageable after all.*

I need to make sure Jon really is okay with what he's offering, especially because of who I want to ask. I never told Jon about my inappropriate attraction to my boss, and now I'm doubly glad I didn't.

"What if I asked Mr. Knight?"

A slow smile blossoms over Jon's face. "Can you see if he'll take a picture of you if he ties you up?"

My brain blips out and I can't respond for a few seconds. I feel my panties grow damp and I fight the urge to squirm. *Oh, hell yes!*

I reply offhandedly. "Sure, I'll ask. Assuming he's even free."

Jon sighs in contentment and closes his eyes while I undo the braid, comb my fingers through his hair, and daydream about my upcoming birthday. Turning 29 doesn't seem so bad now.

# CHAPTER 2

I'm nauseated and second-guessing myself when I cruise into work the next morning. I'm not sure I can follow through with inviting Mr. Knight. The receptionist, Cindy, gives a cheerful hello and I attempt to put enthusiasm in my voice when I parrot it back to her. Cindy is incredibly sweet, but I try to distance myself from her since I'm fucking my four bosses. I don't know what she knows, but I don't want her thinking the bosses are taking advantage of me since I'm a willing participant. It's better if I keep things on a professional level with her.

It's been months now since I started living the hotwife lifestyle after Jon prompted me to try it. I'm more fulfilled than I thought possible. I couldn't imagine going back to straight monogamy, though Jon knows I'll stop this at any point if he says the word. But he's having fun as well, and it invigorated our sex life beyond our wildest dreams, so he has no intention of ending it.

It's a busy day at work, and I'm able to forget most of my troubles until lunchtime. As I'm contemplating whether to eat the leftover lasagna I brought or if I should hit the deli down the street, my instant messenger blinks at me.

My stomach drops when I see it's from Mr. Knight.

*I hear you have a birthday coming up.*

Uh, what? I didn't mention it to anyone at work. Does he have access to my personnel files? I debate for a moment about how to answer, and decide to be cheeky.

*Maybe. Depends on who's asking.*

I chew on my lip as I wait for his reaction. In my anxiety, I'd already eaten off my cherry Chapstick, so it's good I didn't wear lipstick today.

*Your husband emailed me and asked if I wanted to celebrate your birthday with you since he'll be out of town.*

The room spins and my breath catches. Uh, what the fuck did Jon do? I don't know how to respond, but Mr. Knight continues.

*I'm free that night, if you want me.*

Do I want him? Does Raggedy Ann have a cotton crotch? My hands are shaking as I reply.

*I would enjoy some company.*

Bouncing in my seat, I fight to contain a squeal. Oh, my God. He wants to do this! Jon deserves an amazing blowjob before he leaves on his trip. I would have stewed about talking to Mr. Knight for days and possibly lost the nerve. Now it's happening and my birthday is going to be incredible! I'm busy celebrating in my head and almost miss that my IM is flashing at me.

*I put the date on my calendar. Just give me a time and address before then.*

I quickly type back, "Yes, Sir." along with a smiley face emoji, and decide that today is not a leftover lasagna type of day and I deserve lunch at the deli. Glancing at the calendar, I count the days until my birthday. Ugh, 19 more days. How am I going to wait that long? This is worse than when I was a kid waiting for Christmas. I should print out a calendar page with my birthday circled and then every night I can X out a square and watch it get closer and closer.

I snicker softly. Oh, I've got it bad.

# CHAPTER 3

The funny thing is, just because my head is totally full of Mr. Knight doesn't mean that my other bosses aren't also still interested in fucking me. Over time, we've developed a loose schedule where twice a week I'd have a random encounter with someone. It's odd to have a rotating schedule with four men, but Mondays are the busiest days for the law firm, so we all tactfully agree to avoid the distraction on that day. With two encounters per week and four bosses, I'm fucking each one every other week.

As I learn more about their personalities and grow closer to them, it's almost as if I'm dating four men. They all do little things to make me smile. I continued to call them by their last names, despite knowing their first names. I don't want to slip up and become too familiar with them in the office and have Cindy and the paralegal wonder what is going on. Plus, I might have a slight kink about fucking my boss and prefer to keep them in the "boss" category in my mind.

Out of all of them, Mr. Knight thrills me the most sexually, but he isn't the one I bond with intellectually. I am tongue-tied around Mr. Knight and he and I share little conversation when we're together. Usually, I am obedient and do what he tells me to do.

Mr. Daniels is the one I mesh with the best mentally, and we laugh a ton. I never imagined being close to any of them months ago, especially not when I was seducing Mr. Daniels and he was watching me stick his lightsaber up my pussy. So I don't know why it surprises me when Mr. Daniels messages me and invites me for a special meeting in the conference room. It's Friday and I haven't seen him yet this week. With how preoccupied I've been, I didn't think about the other lawyers.

I always look forward to our brief encounters, so when I see the message, I reply, "Be there in 10!" while my stomach does pleasant flips and my heartbeat speeds up.

I don't want to appear to be in a rush, so I stroll casually down the hall. The closer I get to the conference room, the wetter I become. The conference room has a few small windows, and I notice the blinds are already closed. Mr. Daniels is in the chair closet to the door, turned around to face towards me and away from the conference table.

He smiles, winks at me, and commands, "Lock the door."

I giggle and salute him. "Aye aye, Captain."

I click the lock and lean against the door, waiting for him to make the next move. He brought me in here for a reason. We don't normally meet in the conference room, so he must have a plan.

He reclines back in his chair and comments, "You know how there was a big meeting in here earlier?"

"Uh-huh." I nod to emphasize I was paying attention. It was just for the lawyers but it's a small firm, so it's always obvious when all four lawyers are in a meeting at the same time.

"It was boring, but I imagined fucking you on the table to pass the time."

My pussy perks up as I check out the table with more interest. I'm down with this idea. I'm usually bent over something, but this time

I want him on the table with me — it's plenty big enough. Now that he's explained himself, I have no problem taking action.

I walk towards him and bend over and brush my lips across his. He smells faintly of oranges. Did he have one for lunch? Neediness punches me in the gut and I want to straddle him and devour his mouth. He puts his hands at my waist to hold me still and deepens the kiss, coaxing my lips open so our tongues can dance and create a delicious ache in my core.

"Mmm," I moan, and when he cups my breasts as plays with them through my blue blouse, I don't hold back my sigh of pleasure. Mr. Daniels is never rough or demanding with me, and it's all about mutual satisfaction.

Pulling back from him, I stand up and unbutton my blouse. I kick my black flats off my feet and while I undress, Mr. Daniels loosens his tie and unbuttons his shirt. I love how on meeting days, they all dress formally. My pussy gets a pleasant buzz from a man wearing a tie, and now that I've watched all of them remove those ties at various times in the past few months, it's even more erotic when they wear one.

My blouse and black skirt come off quickly and I fold them and lay them on an empty chair. No sense in getting them wrinkled, since I want to walk out of this conference room looking the same as when I walked in. I'm left in my Friday days-of-the-week underpants and a white cotton bra. I still occasionally surprise the lawyers with sexy lingerie, but we've been doing this long enough now that I need to consider comfort. Plus, Mr. Daniels enjoys plain cotton, so this is more of a turn on to him than a matching lace set would be.

I pause while Mr. Daniels removes all his clothes. I enjoy watching the striptease, even if it's not meant to entice. He's fit and attractive, and when he pulls his boxer briefs off, his thick cock springs out, fully erect. I rub my thighs together in anticipation, the moisture gathering at my core. Unhooking my bra, I let it slide down my arms and drop to the floor. My panties join them and I sit on the edge of the conference table. Mr. Daniels pushes my knees apart and stands between them, kissing me and playing with my nipples. *God, he's a great lover.*

I sigh into his mouth and brush my hands along the length of his shaft. I want him inside of me, but he's intent on taking his time today. His cock is wet with pre-cum and I use it as lubrication as I massage him. When he moves a hand to my pussy and slips a finger between my folds to rub my clit, I'm sensitive and his firm touch makes me tense up and whimper. He eases up and caresses me in gentle circles. I relax into it, enjoying the all-over-body tingles.

When he pushes me back on the table but stays standing, I almost protest that I want him to climb up with me, but the tip of his cock against my cave entrance distracts me. When he presses in slowly, his thickness pings all the nerve endings and I groan as he grips my hips and fucks me at a steady pace. My husband is more of a jackrabbit in bed, and I've grown to appreciate Mr. Daniels's thoroughness as he takes his time.

Wrapping my legs around him, I close my eyes and let passion overtake me. Waves of delight wash over me with every thrust. I'm half aware that my moans are loud and I'm continually chanting "Oh, my god," but I'm beyond caring. Mr. Daniels eventually picks up speed, slamming into me roughly and spiraling me over the edge.

I come hard, bucking against him while he drills into me. My "Oh god," turns into a long "Ooooooh," as my pussy quivers and milks his cock. Mr. Daniels isn't far behind me, and he cries out when he erupts. He once told me that watching me come is what gets him off, and I believe him since he's never gotten there before me.

We're both panting as we descend from the peak. When he pulls out, my legs go limp and I'm in too awkward a position to relax in.

He helps me sit up and then swivels a chair around, scoops me up into his arms, and sits down with me cuddled against him.

I rest against him for several minutes, both of us silent and enjoying the moment. I'm content and thinking about how sex is different with each boss, when he finally breaks the silence.

"We should probably get back to work."

*Bleh, he's right.* I sigh in response and climb out of his lap. We kiss a few times as we're getting dressed.

I want to make sure he knows I appreciate all the effort he makes with me, so I murmur against his lips after one of our kisses. "That was fantastic today. Thank you."

He smiles and brushes his mouth against my forehead. "Miranda, you know I think you're amazing, right?"

His words warm me, but also make me shy. He's generous with his compliments and I should be used to it by now, but it still takes me by surprise. I blush and try to make light of his comments. "Yes, but it's always nice to hear."

Once we're done dressing, he cleans the conference table with a sanitizing wipe. We embrace and hug for a moment, and he holds my hand until we leave the room.

When we part ways, I pause and watch him walking the opposite direction. He's never mentioned a girlfriend or wife, and I'm curious why he's single. *Jesus, he's going to make someone happy someday.*

# CHAPTER 4

I take Jon to the airport the night before my birthday. His work wants him to take the weekend to get settled in because they have a long week of meetings ahead of them. I make no promises to call him after Mr. Knight leaves, but tell him I'll text him at the end of the night and let him know everything is fine. We make plans to have a long talk on the phone the next day so I can give him all the juicy details. Jon pouts a tad when I explain there will be no bondage picture, but I agree to let him try more elaborate bondage with me and then he can take his own dang photo.

It's rare for Jon to make trips without me, so the house is too quiet when I get back home. I build a blanket and pillow bed on the couch and curl up to watch a light romcom Christmas movie. The mindless entertainment keeps me from stressing about tomorrow night with Mr. Knight. When I fall asleep halfway through the movie and wake up when the show is over, I turn the TV off, snuggle into the pillows and try to doze off again. No reason to make the bed for only a few hours of sleep.

I was smart and planned in advance, making sure my Saturday morning and afternoon are full, so I won't pace around the house with excess energy and psych myself out for the upcoming night. I booked an early manicure and pedicure, and when I leave the saloon with pink fingernails and toes, they give me the confidence boost I need to feel sexy and feminine. Next stop is a department store with a great selection of lingerie. I have a strong preference for black, but I give myself credit for at least mulling over other color options. A slinky, black one-piece bodysuit and new thigh-highs catch my eye and I don't cringe at the total cost like usual. Lingerie is so dang expensive, but it's my birthday and I'm worth it.

Mr. Knight is coming over at 6 p.m., and he texted me last night to tell me to eat a light dinner beforehand and that he'll feed me after he's done with me. The wording of the message sent shivers of delight down my spine. After he's done with me... *fuck, that's hot.* I take him at his word and eat a salad at 5 p.m., despite not feeling hungry, and then spend the rest of the time getting dressed in my new lingerie and braiding my hair so it's out of the way.

Inviting Mr. Knight over changes the dynamic of our encounter. I've never shagged any of the bosses outside of work, and I don't know what to expect. What if this is a horrible idea? If something bad happens, it could ruin our working relationship. What if he hurts me unintentionally? Maybe I should call this off. My brain pictures several unlikely but horrible situations, and I'm woozy when the doorbell rings.

I don't put on any shoes, and my stocking feet are silent on the floor as I head towards the front door. There is no way for him to know I'm on the other side, and I use the peephole to verify it's him. I pause and don't open it. What should I tell him? I jump when he rings the bell again, and he also knocks this time. *Ugh, I better just let him in.* Taking a deep breath, I crack the door open.

A bouquet of pink Gerber daisies is thrust at me and I can't help but smile. *Shit, he remembers my favorite flower.*

"Happy birthday, Kitten."

My heart warms at the pet name, and I stand aside so he can enter. Mr. Knight is wearing jeans and a grey t-shirt. I've only seen him out of a suit a couple times a year at the company picnic, and his sexiness punches me in the gut.

I'm flushed and can't meet his eyes. "I'll go put these in water."

He's carrying another grocery bag, and he follows me into the kitchen. It's weird to be the one being celebrated and wished happy birthday when the door opens. So many times it was me on the other side wishing someone else a happy day before I fucked them.

Mr. Knight breaks my train of thought. "Mind if I put some food in the fridge?"

I mumble, "Oh, no, go ahead," while I fetch a vase from under the sink and fill it with water. I arrange the flowers to my liking and admire my artwork. I'm working at an L-shaped counter, and the fridge is behind me. I hear the rustling in the fridge stop, and he comes up and presses into my ass, circling his arms around my waist.

He nuzzles my neck and inhales. "Mmm, you smell delicious—like coconut—and look so sexy."

My heart pounds at his compliment and my pussy gets wet. I want to babble about my conditioner smelling like coconuts and my shopping trip, but hold my tongue. I'm glad he appreciates the new purchase, but if I'm going to tell him to leave, I better do it now.

Mr. Knight reaches out and picks up the vase with one hand. "Here, why don't I take this."

He's still squeezed against me, so I'm trapped between him and the counter, but I turn my head and watch him place the vase out of the way on the opposite L-side surface. I only have a moment to wonder why he set it over there when the hand on my waist slides down my front and rubs my pussy through the bodysuit.

My breath catches while I moan and instinctively spread my legs to give him better access. His fingers ignite a fire in my core, and he's barely started. *Um, yeah, I'm not telling him to leave.*

I grind against his hardness through his jeans. I squeak in surprise when he pushes me over the counter, ass up. *Oooh, okay. Guess we're doing something here.* He said he had plans, but I didn't envision them including anything in the kitchen.

Both his hands explore my crease through the fabric, one finger pulling at the edge of the suit and running a finger underneath it. What he's doing tickles, so I wiggle my ass at him and giggle. I'm rewarded with a slap on my pussy that makes me gasp. *Sweet Jesus, he's starting in with what I like early.* My head spins when I realize I'm willing to do whatever he asks tonight. I'm his for the taking.

"Miranda?"

I'm so concentrated on his fingers rubbing me, that I'm spacey and dreamy when I reply. "Hmm?"

Mr. Knight stops moving his hand. "Miranda, pay attention for a moment."

I struggle to clear the fog. "Okay. I'm focused." I'm half lying, but I'm clear enough to hold a conversation.

"Kitten, tonight you can call me by my first name or Sir, but nothing else. Okay?"

His words sober me all the way. Uh, he wants me to call him Nick—or wait, his full name is Nicholas, but he goes by Nick. Which one does he want?

My reply indicates my preferred term. "Okay, Nick—I mean, Sir."

Nick chuckles at my response before continuing. "Also, Kitten, if you are uncomfortable with anything, use the stoplight colors like we've done before. Okay?"

*Ooooh.* This means he's planning on doing something I might ask him to stop. My pussy clenches in anticipation.

"Yes, Sir."

He sighs out, "Good girl," while he unsnaps the crotch of my bodysuit. The cool air hits my heated, wet pussy, and when his fingers probe my velvety folds, I lose focus on everything except the pleasure as he caresses my clit.

When the room spins, I close my eyes and lay my head on the counter, gripping the edge with both hands in case this turns rough. You never know with Nick. My pussy aches and I desperately want him to fill me, but I will not ask for it tonight. If he has a plan, I want to let this play out and see where it goes.

My stomach flutters when his belt buckle clinks and his zipper opens. A couple dull thuds on the linoleum have me guessing that he kicked his shoes off. He's barely been in the door for 15 minutes and I'm about to be railed in my kitchen. This is wonderfully slutty.

"So Kitten, you have a choice tonight."

*Wait, I have options?* "Yes?" I almost giggle at how breathy I sound. There is no hiding how turned on I am.

"Since it's your birthday, what would you like me to call you tonight?"

*What's this?* Lifting my head off the counter, I peek over my shoulder at him, but he's examining my pussy instead of looking at my face. I flush at how exposed I am. I didn't think he'd be memorizing every detail while he was back there. Fighting the urge to stand up and cover myself, I shuffle my feet and swallow a lump in my throat while still watching him.

There is only one thing I want to be called by him, other than Kitten. "Call me a slut."

He stops studying my exposed bits and flashes me an evil grin. "Okay, Slut, here is what is going to happen —"

I get a kick from the world 'slut' and my pussy throbs. I lower my head to the counter again as he goes on.

"I'm going to fuck you right here for five minutes, but you aren't allowed to come."

*Um, what's this?* How am I supposed to stop myself from coming if he's the one fucking me? I'm about to argue with him, but he continues again.

"If you think you are going to come, tell me. If you don't tell me and you come, you won't like what happens afterwards."

*Oh, fuck.* My brain stops working, and I freeze for a moment. My senses turn back on with a whoosh, and my entire body flushes and I tremble. Curling my toes against the floor, my pussy quivers against his hand as he gently circles my wet hole with two fingers, not pressing in.

"Do you understand, Slut?"

He emphasizes his words with a hard thrust of the fingers into my cunt, and I squeak in shock from the pleasurable pain.

I gasp out a "Yes!" as he removes his hand and drills his cock straight to my core. I groan out long and loud. "Oh, my god."

Nick sets a rapid pace, ramming me against the counter with every inward plunge. Pleasure rushes through me as my cave massages the length of him, but I don't think I'm at the risk of coming. Everything he's doing is amazing, and I eagerly push my ass back towards him, greedy for his cock every time he pulls out, and I ache for him to use me roughly.

When it looks as if he's going to keep the same pace for the whole five minutes, I request, "Mmm, fuck me harder, Sir."

"No," he bites out harshly.

*Uh, what?* I don't know if he's ever said no to me before.

I whimper. "Please?"

My chest tightens when he lets out an unamused laugh. My mouth goes dry and my heart races, while he chides, "Slut, I will fuck you however I want. You don't have a choice. Do you understand?"

"Oh, god, yes," I say this through gritted teeth as he continues the same pace.

My head spins with a kaleidoscope of thoughts. Did I order domination for my birthday? I thought I was just going to get tied up for some kinky fun, but maybe this is how he is out of the office? His insistence on me knowing I can use the stop-light safe words makes sense now. A buzz in my brain turns to ringing in my ears and my legs almost give out. *Do I want this?*

I grip the counter tighter and use the leverage to push back against him even harder, meeting his every thrust to force him in deeper. His cock hits my most sensitive spot, and the uncontrollable lust decides for me. *Oh yeah, I want this.* My chest loosens and I can breathe easier. I'm ready to be fucked up.

Nick pulls out fully and I slump against the counter. Already my legs are like Jell-O and this was only five minutes. I still can't believe he's been at my house for less than half an hour, and we've already progressed to this point. I'm going to be a wet mess by the time he's done with me.

He orders, "Stand up and turn around."

I don't reply, but do as he commands while he digs around in the bag he left on the counter. I didn't realize he'd removed all his clothes, but he's buck naked and I admire his ass. *Mmm, he's got that fit dad vibe going on.*

When he pulls out a pair of handcuffs, my eyes widen while my pussy twitches and my nipples pucker. *Oh, hell yes.*

"Bring your hands together in front of you."

I whisper, "Yes, Sir," while holding my arms out close together.

He clasps the handcuffs on me and tugs on the links between them, forcing me to stumble forward.

"Follow," he commands, and I dutifully follow him into the hallway as he keeps one hand on the cuffs so he can lead me.

*Where in the hell is he taking me?* He doesn't know the layout of my house. When he heads towards the front door, I slow my walk and he tugs on the cuffs. *Uh, what the fuck is he doing?* There is no way in hell I'm letting him take me outside so that my neighbor Harold and his wife Vickie will get an eyeful of my BDSM birthday adventure. I don't care if I already fucked Harold for his birthday. I'm private with my kinks. Plus, there are other families with kids in my neighborhood.

I'm about to use the safe word when he stops just before he gets to the door. I'm confused as he reaches up and pulls on the hooks of a coat rack bolted to the wall. He seems satisfied with something and grins at me before snatching all the coats and tossing them to the ground.

"Hey!" I protest while a flash of annoyance zips through me.

*What the fuck does he think he's doing?* I'm going to have to clean those up later. When he grabs my wrists and lifts my arms to hook the cuffs around one knob on the coat rack, I realize his intent was always obvious and I was the imperceptive one.

"Stay here," he warns, and disappears down the hall into the kitchen.

I'm tall enough that my feet are flat on the floor. I snicker and test that I can easily lift my wrists off the hook. If he wants the illusion of me being stuck, I'm willing to oblige, but I could easily free myself from this position.

When he returns with something in his hand, I realize it's a bundle of zip ties as he uses them to fasten the handcuffs securely to the hook. He pulls on my wrists to make sure that the cuffs now can't slide off the end and then stands back to admire his handiwork.

He sounds bored when he says, "I'm thirsty, so I'm going to go get a drink and check my emails. I'll be back."

I'm speechless and my eyes widen as he walks back to the kitchen. I test that I can't get the cuffs off the end of the hook, and I remember the day Jon installed this coat rack, and I know he was very thorough in making sure it wouldn't come off the wall. He was using a stud finder and swearing up a storm while trying to find the perfect size of bit for his drill. *He can't just leave me here like this, can he?*

A few minutes pass while I ponder what to do. How long does it take someone to get a glass of water and check their emails? I heard kitchen cupboards opening while he was presumably hunting for a glass, and the tap water turned on, so I know he got his drink.

My pulse speeds up and my body tenses the longer I wait, and a wave of indignation hits me. This is my birthday, and it's supposed to be fun. Standing in the hallway with my arms secured above my head isn't my idea of a good time. The buzz from my displeasure reaches my cooch and wetness trickles down my thigh. *Sure, my slutty pussy is all into this, of course.*

I sigh heavily and flex my fingers. This position is getting uncomfortable, but I'm sure he'll be back any minute. I better get a good hard fucking for being such a good girl. I know I could call out the safe word and he'd hear it. There is nowhere in my house that I couldn't reach with a good yell, but I'm not at that point yet.

If I'm being honest, the longer I wait, the more turned on I'm getting. *Fuck. Being at the mercy of his whim is hot.* I know that's why he did this, and I semi hate that I'm responding to it, but my other half doesn't care. My pussy will wait as long as it takes to get fucked against this wall while I'm helpless.

At some point I lose track of time and mentally zone out. Nick needs to come back and ravish me. My inner thighs are a damp mess from my dripping pussy, and my hard nipples ache. I've gone through the whole gamut of emotions since he left me; from anger to frustration, desperation, and now acceptance.

I'm mentally floating in this odd dream-like fuzzy state where time has no meaning and everything is calm and peaceful. When the air conditioner kicks on, it sounds extra loud and the cool breeze blowing across my skin sends ripples of pleasure through me. I giggle at how stupid it is that blowing air can feel this nice. Does it always feel this lovely? How have I never noticed it before except on extremely hot days?

What would Nick do if I called out to him? Would Stern Daddy come and punish me? I smile at the thought. Yep, let's see what happens.

"Sir?" I call out, ignoring the temptation to call him Daddy. He only gave me two options on what to use for his name tonight and I want him to fuck me, so I better not anger him.

What felt like a split second later, he turns the corner in the hallway and stops to look at me.

"Yes, Slut?"

Wait, was he coming back to me or did I space out? Didn't I just say his name and now he's here? I snicker at myself. Does it matter?

I can barely keep a straight face. "Um, I'm ready to be fucked."

"Oh, are you now?" He sounds amused.

I vow solemnly. "Yes, Sir. My pussy is ready for you."

I'm not sure I've ever said my pussy was ready for anything before, not aloud, but the trance-like calm also includes a willingness to say stuff I wouldn't normally say. I'd probably tell him anything if I thought it would get his cock inside of me.

He walks towards me. "I'll be the judge of that," and forces my legs apart with his knee and slips his fingers into my pussy.

I arch against him and moan. Oh, fuck. His fingers are amazing. I grind against his hand and strain at the binds on my wrist. I want to force his fingers in deeper somehow.

Nick laughs. "Yes, I think you're ready."

He lifts me up by my hips so he can fit his cock against my sopping wet hole. When he rams into me, I'm forced back against the wall and I squeal from the intense sensation. As he drills into me, I chant, "Fuck me," repeatedly, and I toss in some other nasty things that he might like. I don't really know what I'm saying, but I think at one point I tell him to pound my pussy, and to fuck me like he means it. Whatever I'm saying must be fine, because he continues to fuck me hard.

I'm so worked up, his sharp thrusts quickly edge me towards my orgasm. I hook my legs around his sides and explode violently, screaming out and bucking wildly against his cock. Quaking against him, I barely notice that he wedges me against the wall, pressing into me hard so that he can keep me steady while he reaches up to fiddle with the zip ties. The pressure of his body and my legs still wrapped around him keeps me from falling as he unhooks me from the coat rack.

I'm drifting in a sea of bliss as he pulls his cock out and carries me to the living room. He lays me on my back on the rug in front of the fireplace, spreads my legs, and slides back into me. I moan as he fucks me hard and fast. I can tell this isn't for my benefit, and he's fucking me so he can come, but it doesn't stop me from spiraling into ecstasy again.

The room spins as I shudder and cry out with my second orgasm. Nick's full body weight presses into me as he jerks and groans with release. The room fades away as I come down from my peak, and I'm back to drifting in a happy, warm place, totally sated.

Everything feels far away, and when he rolls off of me, I barely notice. My eyes are closed and he tugs me to his side, cuddling me as our harsh breathing slows down. We're both slick with sweat, but I don't care.

When he moves away and gets up, I mewl in protest.

"I'll be right back, Kitten. You need water."

I melt into the floor while he's gone. Maybe I'll just live right here, never moving. I blink and he's putting a glass of water in my hand.

"Drink."

I struggle up on my elbows to take a sip and Nick holds me steady. The cool water helps shake me from my sexual daze. I glance over at him as he settles down, sitting cross-legged next to me, and picks up a Chinese food to-go container. My stomach rumbles and I realize I'm ravenous. I sit up all the way, mimicking his pose and touching knees with him.

He hands me a container and a fork and I dig into a cold noodle and chicken dish. I don't know what it is, but it's delicious. I giggle at how ridiculous we look, both naked and eating cold takeout on the floor, but I don't think I would have it any other way. This is a pretty fabulous birthday.

We talk about inane things for a few minutes while we eat. He complains about being overly stressed lately, which I didn't realize he was. I tell him the juicy details of Chloe's recent birthday, though I don't tell him her name to protect her privacy.

I can't eat the entire container, and set it aside when I suddenly don't feel well. Something is off and when I look down at my hands, they are visibly shaking. I look at Nick, wide-eyed, and he sets the leftovers on a side table and scoops me up in his arms and carries me to the couch. He sets me down briefly, retrieves the water glass, and comes back to me.

He puts the glass under my nose. "Drink again."

I take a sip and he says, "Good girl," while setting the glass on the side table next to the food containers. He lies down on the couch, forcing me down with him so we're spooning. I'm my favorite little spoon, but I don't get time to enjoy it because I shake harder. Nick rubs my back and arms, and kisses my neck occasionally, but I don't want to talk much because I'm afraid my teeth will rattle.

"Miranda, how do you feel?"

I murmur, "Weird, floating. This happened with Alec."

Nick snickers and sounds like he's talking to himself. "Alec always did like to play hard."

He smooths some strands of hair that came loose from the braid and continues to rub my back.

"I think you might have been in subspace. Do you know what that is?"

I think back to Jon rambling on about his BDSM research and how he explained some stuff to me, but I didn't think it would pertain to me so I didn't pay too much attention, but I remember him talking about subspace because it sounded so odd.

"Yeah, I've heard of it."

I don't have the energy to explain any further.

"Miranda, can I stay the night? I don't want to leave you alone."

His request wakes me up a little. Oh, shit. I never considered that possibility, but a yearning to have him stay hits me, so I answer without thinking it through.

"Yes."

He responds, "Good," and a few seconds later with, "Thank you," and it warms my heart.

We continue to lie there and eventually doze. I wake briefly when he carries me to the master bedroom and we snuggle into bed together. My last thought before falling asleep is wondering if Jon is going to be pissed.

# CHAPTER 5

Oh yeah, Jon's pissed. But not because Nick stayed the night. The anger has to do with the fact I forgot to text him before bed and he spent an anxious night worrying about me. I'm frantically messaging Jon while Nick makes us bacon and eggs for breakfast. I promise Jon I'll call him the moment Nick leaves, and I set my phone down to concentrate on my last bit of time with Nick.

I'm wearing only a bathrobe, and Nick is only in his jeans. He looks mighty fine in them. When the food is ready, we eat and chat about nothing important, but I'm breathless and buzzing just being close to him. At one point he smiles at me and my heart leaps into my throat. *Oh fuck, this isn't good.*

After breakfast, he gathers his stuff to head out. I walk him to the door, still in my bathrobe, and we share a long, passionate kiss.

"Have a good day Miranda, and happy birthday again."

I smile softly at him and thank him. Pulling my robe closed and cinching the knot tighter, I open the door so he can leave. I wait in the doorway and wave at him as he drives off before stepping back and closing it.

When I walk into the kitchen, I plop down into a chair at the table and stare at the wall. I'm so fucked. I think I'm in love with my boss.

Needing time to gather my thoughts, I don't call Jon immediately. There is no way in hell I'm telling Jon I've developed feelings for Nick. I don't want to stop seeing him. I just need to figure out how to make it so I don't ruin everything. Nick can't know what I feel... ever.

I settle down once I decide to ignore how I'm feeling and pretend everything is normal. I push the craziness aside and focus on my amazing birthday. This really was one of my best birthdays ever. Jon is going to need to up his game for my 30th. I snicker when I think of how I can leverage this for a blow-out birthday next year.

I call and smooth things over with Jon and later that night I'm lying in bed and realize that I didn't have any cake. *Well, that's dumb.* I know exactly what I would have wished for. Do wishes come true if they aren't made on your birthday? I decide a person gets one wish for their birthday and the exact date doesn't matter since plenty of people celebrate on a different day.

Before I fall asleep, I set my alarm early so I can stop and buy cupcakes before work. *I'm getting my wish, goddamit*!

The End

Want more?<br>
Get a bundle of erotic shorts featuring Miranda. Including:<br>
"Cleaning up After the Boss"<br>
"Taking Dictation From the Boss"<br>
"Being Bent Over My Boss's Desk and Forced to Apologize"<br>
Find it at https://lacey-cross.com/fourlawyers

# About Lacey Cross

I'm mainly a writer who got bored during the pandemic and turned to erotica out of desperation. I found out I love the creativity and challenge of self-publishing sexy stories. I write a variety of kinks, but most are wife sharing with a touch of BDSM power control.

Connect with me at:

https://lacey-cross.com/

# Acknowledgments

No book of mine would be complete without thanking my editor. She's the reason I started writing, and she's been my biggest supporter.

*Wordcat, thank you for everything you've done for me!*